D0197616

THE SPONGEBOB MOVIE
SPONGE OUT OF WATER

THE JUNIOR NOVELIZATION

Based on the original screenplay by
Stephen Hillenburg, Paul Tibbitt,
Jonathan Aibel, and Glenn Berger

Adapted by David Lewman

Random House 🏠 New York

created by

Stephen Hillenburg

ISBN 978-0-385-38775-0

randomhousekids.com

Printed in the United States of America

10 9 8 7 6 5 4 3 2 1

In the middle of the bright blue ocean, a pirate ship sat anchored just off the shore of a tiny desert island. Burger Beard, the captain of the ship, eagerly rowed a little wooden boat to the beach.

The moment the tip of his boat touched the sand, he jumped out, carrying a map and his trusty sword. "At long last," he said greedily. "The legendary treasure will be mine!"

Following the map, Burger Beard hacked his way through the thick jungle to the ruins of an ancient temple. At the far end of the temple, a dusty pirate skeleton sat on a magnificent throne, holding an old leather-bound book.

When he saw the book, Burger Beard's eyes lit up. "Thar ye be, me lovely!" he whispered. Dancing a happy jig, he made his way across the temple to the throne. Then he cupped his ear and pretended to listen to the silent pirate skeleton.

"Oh, what's that?" he asked. "Take the book? I don't mind if I do!"

He yanked the old book out of the skeleton's hand, and the skeleton collapsed into a pile of bones. If Burger Beard hadn't been so busy kissing the book, he might have heard a strange sound, like mechanical gears turning and grinding. . . .

ZWHEET! ZWHEET! ZWHEET! Poison darts flew straight at Burger Beard!

But the pirate didn't notice. He was twirling around, hugging the book to his chest. "It's mine! Finally, you are MINE!"

Lucky for the greedy pirate, hundreds of poison darts zipped past, missing him. Giant spikes shot up through the floor of the temple, but none of them skewered Burger Beard. When he had finished his joyful dance with the book, he bowed and a huge spike pierced his hat, narrowly missing his head.

Burger Beard stood up straight, adjusted his hat, and started to leave with the book.

Then someone tapped him on the shoulder.

When he turned around, he saw the pirate skeleton! It had reassembled itself, and now it was waving its bony fists, challenging Burger Beard to a fight.

"Bring it on, Skinny," Burger Beard said, laughing. "You don't scare me!"

CRACK! The skeleton landed a tremendous punch right on Burger Beard's chin, which sent him flying all the way back to his ship. *THUMP!* The pirate landed hard on the deck.

He bounced up and shook his fist at the island. "Is that all ya got?" he jeered. He kissed the book one more time, weighed anchor, caught a good stiff wind, and sailed away.

Satisfied with his course, Burger Beard hit the auto-pirate button on the ship's steering wheel and sat down in his reading chair. As he opened the ancient volume, several curious seagulls settled around him to listen.

"Let's see," he muttered. "How does this story begin?"

He began to read out loud. "'Once upon a time under the sea, there was a little town called Bikini Bottom. In this town, there was a place called the Krusty Krab, where folks would come to eat a thing called a Krabby Patty.'"

The seagulls smiled. They liked this story already!

"'Every greasy spoon has a fry cook,'" Burger Beard continued, "'and the one who worked here went by the name of SpongeBob SquarePants. He loved making Krabby Patties, and the good citizens of Bikini Bottom loved eating them, despite their doctors' warnings.'"

"Why did the citizens wuv eating Kwabby Patties so much, Mistew Piwate?" asked the littlest seagull, whose name was Kyle.

Burger Beard looked up from the book. "Well, Kyle, it says right here in the book that it was a secret!"

"Ooh, I WUV secwets!" Kyle said.

Burger Beard resumed reading. "'No one was sure what was in these patties that made them so delicious. And frankly, no one cared. No one except a tiny guy named Plankton.'"

Kyle leaned over the pirate's shoulder to stare at the picture of Plankton in the book. In the drawing, Plankton was holding on to the handle of a safe while SpongeBob tried to vacuum him off it.

"'Plankton had made it his life's work to steal the Krabby Patty recipe,'" Burger Beard read. "'But SpongeBob was always there to protect it. On this particular day, though, things would be different. . . .'"

CHAPTER 2

High above Bikini Bottom, a bomber plane flew toward the Krusty Krab. Behind the restaurant, SpongeBob tossed a bag into the trash bin just as his best friend, Patrick, walked up.

"Good morning, SpongeBob!" Patrick said cheerfully.

"Good morning, Patrick!" SpongeBob answered. "Are you here for your pre-lunch Krabby Patty?"

"I'm thinking TWO today! One for me . . . and one for my friend!"

"Oh!" SpongeBob said. "Have I met this friend?"

Patrick used both hands to squish his belly to look like a big mouth. He moved his hands to make the "mouth" talk. "You know ME, SpongeBob!"

The two pals laughed. "Enjoy, Patrick's tummy!" SpongeBob said.

Up above the Krusty Krab, the bomber plane

dropped a huge jar of tartar sauce. As the gigantic jar fell, it made a whistling sound.

Meanwhile, in front of the Krusty Krab, the owner, Mr. Krabs, was happily counting the customers who were lining up to spend their money. He was too busy counting to notice the whistle of the falling jar. "Thirteen, fourteen, fifteen . . ."

SpongeBob went over to his boss. "Hey, Mr. Krabs," he said. "I thought we got our tartar sauce delivery on Thursday."

Mr. Krabs stopped counting. Puzzled, he asked, "Tartar . . ."

SPLAT! The giant jar hit the ground and exploded, covering everyone and everything with tartar sauce!

". . . sauce?" Mr. Krabs finished as tartar sauce dripped off his nose and claws.

Overhead, the pilot of the bomber plane circled around to see the damage he had done. Mr. Krabs and SpongeBob heard a familiar voice yell, "Bull's-eye!" and laugh evilly. The plane flew off.

"Plankton!" cried SpongeBob, recognizing the evil laugh right away.

"So it's a food fight he wants, eh?" Mr. Krabs said, determined. He grabbed SpongeBob and said, "Listen up, boy! Plankton's tried to steal me formuler thousands of times, but he's never had a PLANE before! So protect the secret formuler AT ALL COSTS!"

SpongeBob saluted and started to hurry inside to defend the Krabby Patty secret formula. Mr. Krabs realized what he had just said. "But not ACTUAL COSTS," he added. "You know what I mean. To yer battle stations!"

Plankton piloted his bomber plane toward the Krusty Krab for another attack. "Welcome to Air Plankton!" he announced to no one in particular, enjoying himself. "Please put your seat backs and tray tables up, as we're now approaching our final destination. . . ."

Up on the roof of the Krusty Krab, a giant anti-aircraft gun rose into position. SpongeBob and Patrick, wearing their battle helmets, worked the gun.

"Okay, Patrick!" SpongeBob yelled. "Load the potatoes!"

Patrick held up a plate full of steaming potatoes. "Mashed or scalloped, sir?"

"No, Patrick," SpongeBob said. "RAW!"

"Sir, yes, sir!" Patrick answered, saluting. He dropped the plate of cooked potatoes, picked up a bag of raw potatoes, and poured them into the antiaircraft gun. "Locked and loaded!" he reported.

In his office, Mr. Krabs opened his safe and placed the Krabby Patty secret formula inside. "Don't worry, little formuler!" he said. "You'll be safe in this, uh, safe." He slammed the door closed, twirled the dial, and grabbed a microphone. "FIRE!" he shouted.

On the roof, SpongeBob pulled the trigger. *BLAM! BLAM! BLAM! BLAM! BLAM!* The anti-aircraft gun fired whole potatoes at Plankton's fighter plane.

"POTATOES?" Plankton yelled when he saw them coming straight at him. He pulled the stick to the right, swerving the plane out of the way, and headed toward the Krusty Krab.

"He's closing in!" SpongeBob called.

Patrick peered through a pair of binoculars . . . which he was holding backward. "I think we have a few minutes before he gets here," he said calmly. SpongeBob reached up and flipped the binoculars around. "HE'S RIGHT ON TOP OF US!" Patrick screamed.

SpongeBob kept firing the big gun, but the propellers of Plankton's plane shredded the potatoes into French fries.

"It's gonna take a lot more than potatoes to bring THIS baby down!" Plankton gloated. But just then, the potatoes knocked the wings off his plane. The plane plummeted to the ground and crashed. *WHAM!*

SpongeBob and Patrick celebrated on the roof with a victory dance. "We did it! Woo-hoo!" shouted SpongeBob.

"Yeah! In your FACE, Plankton!" Patrick said.

Then SpongeBob spotted something floating gently through the sky: a parachute. "Wait a minute, Patrick," he said. "Look!"

Dangling from the parachute was a tank. "He's got a tank!" SpongeBob cried.

Inside the tank, Plankton loaded a pickle as ammunition and manned the controls. "Well, Krabs," he said, "you're certainly in a pickle now!" He laughed at his own terrible pun.

The tank shot the pickle at the Krusty Krab. It hit the restaurant and exploded, blowing SpongeBob and Patrick off the roof. They screamed as they fell, but after they hit ground, they stood up, breathing hard. They saw the tank rolling closer!

SpongeBob frantically cranked a field radio and shouted into it. "Your orders, sir?"

From his office, Mr. Krabs answered, "EXTRA KETCHUP! EXTRA MUSTARD! HOLD THE MAYO!"

"Yes, sir!" SpongeBob called, hoisting giant squeeze bottles onto his shoulders.

Patrick lifted a giant jar of mayo over his head. "Hold . . . the . . . mayo!" he grunted. His arms shook with the effort of holding the huge jar over his head. He and SpongeBob watched as the tank rolled closer and closer. . . .

CHAPTER 3

"I can't hold this mayo much longer!" Patrick gasped.

"Wait for the order, soldier!" barked SpongeBob.

Finally, their radio crackled and Mr. Krabs shouted, "Unleash the condiments!"

"With relish!" SpongeBob cried as he shot ketchup and mustard at Plankton's tank. But the tank just kept on coming, firing exploding pickles at the Krusty Krab. Patrick heaved the giant jar of mayo right in front of the tank. *CRASH!*

"MAYO?" Plankton said. "It's gonna take a lot more than MAYO to stop—"

BOOM! The tank ran into the mayo and exploded, sending globs of white goo flying everywhere.

"Oh, mayo . . . ," Patrick said fondly, "is there no problem you can't solve?"

But SpongeBob was carefully watching the wreckage of Plankton's tank. He saw movement. "NOW what?" he asked.

SpongeBob watched in horror as a giant metal robot rose from the smoldering ashes of the tank. Plankton was working the robot's controls from a seat inside its head. He laughed a long, loud, evil laugh and pushed on a control stick. The robot stomped forward. *BOOM! BOOM! BOOM!* The ground shook with every step the giant robot took.

Patrick stared up at the robot. He took off his helmet and handed it to SpongeBob. "I just remembered," he said. "I don't work for Mr. Krabs." He ran off.

SpongeBob dropped the helmet and sprinted for the front door of the Krusty Krab, yelling, "Robot! Robot! ROBOT! ROBOT! GIANT ROBOT!" The terrifying robot chased him.

Inside his office, Mr. Krabs was staring at the closed door. He could hear the thundering steps of the robot coming closer and closer. He could also hear SpongeBob screaming, "ROBOT! ROBOT!"

SpongeBob burst into the office and slammed the door shut behind him. "Mr. Krabs!" he said breathlessly. "Plankton's here and he's got a giant robot!"

"Quick, boy!" Mr. Krabs responded. "Bar the door!"

SpongeBob shoved a flimsy chair under the doorknob. "Got it!" he said, satisfied.

The robot burst through the door and the wall

surrounding it. *SMASH!* It flattened SpongeBob and stomped right up to Mr. Krabs. "I'll take one secret formula," Plankton demanded. "To go!"

The robot's big mechanical hand reached toward Mr. Krabs, who cowered and groaned, until suddenly . . .

. . . the robot sputtered and froze.

Mr. Krabs uncovered his head and looked up, puzzled. "Eh?" he said. SpongeBob peeled himself off the floor and stood up, wondering what the robot was doing.

Inside the robot's head, Plankton stared at a gauge. The needle pointed to *E*. "Oh, BARNACLES!" Plankton cursed. "I'm out of gas!"

He opened a little door, climbed out of the robot's head, and walked down its extended arm to Mr. Krabs. "I'm not through yet!" he vowed. "I've got something that'll make you hand over that formula . . . something you CAN'T resist!"

Mr. Krabs folded his arms and smiled. "And just what would that irresistible thing be, Plankton?"

Plankton whipped out his wallet. Mr. Krabs gasped. "Money!" he wheezed.

"That's right, Krabs!" Plankton said, grinning. "I'll BUY the formula from you!"

SpongeBob grabbed Mr. Krabs's arm and

desperately tried to pull him away from Plankton. "No, Mr. Krabs!" he cried. "Don't do it!"

"No, I won't," Mr. Krabs said. "Of course not." But then he asked, "How much?"

"One . . . dollar," Plankton offered.

"Sold," Mr. Krabs said.

SpongeBob gasped.

"YES!" cried Plankton triumphantly.

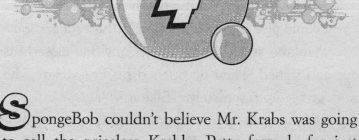

CHAPTER 4

SpongeBob couldn't believe Mr. Krabs was going to sell the priceless Krabby Patty formula for just one dollar! Swaggering over his long-awaited victory, Plankton opened his wallet.

It was empty.

Plankton's eye bulged in disbelief. "That's . . . that's . . . that's IMPOSSIBLE!" he yelled. "It was full of money just last week!"

He thought hard about where all his money could possibly have gone. "But then I bought that airplane. And that tank. And built that giant robot. I knew I shouldn't have put in such a nice seat. But I love comfort. . . ."

Mr. Krabs chuckled. "Sounds to me like someone's just a wee bit broke!"

Plankton shrugged. "Well, Krabs, I guess you've won. I've spent every penny I've ever made trying to put you out of business."

He pulled out a single penny.

"Except this one," Plankton said. "My last penny. What can I do with one measly cent, anyway?"

Mr. Krabs looked at the penny and licked his lips. "You could give it to me," he said. "Just a suggestion."

Plankton stared at his last penny. He closed his eye and sighed. Then he opened his eye. "Here," he said, giving up completely. "Take it."

He tossed the penny to Mr. Krabs, who caught it with one eager claw. Mr. Krabs kissed the penny. Then he opened his safe, tossed the penny inside, and whispered, "Welcome home, little penny. Welcome home." He closed the safe gently.

Plankton began to sob. "You've taken everything else! You might as well take my last penny!"

Mr. Krabs frowned. "You already gave it to me. And no take-backs!"

Huge tears flowed from Plankton's single eye. Mr. Krabs picked him up and carried him out of his office, stopping in the restaurant's dining area. SpongeBob followed his boss.

Holding Plankton in his big claw, Mr. Krabs said, "Well, Plankton, like a reheated Krabby Patty, you've been foiled again!"

He dropped the tiny villain onto the floor. *"Oof!"* Plankton grunted.

"I guess this means the secret formula is safe forever!" SpongeBob said happily. "Right, Mr. Krabs?"

Mr. Krabs nodded. "It sure does, boy."

Plankton let out a big sigh.

"Why don't you scurry along, Plankton?" Mr. Krabs said. "I've got a successful business to run." He and the customers laughed. Plankton gave another sob, hung his little green head, and slunk out of the Krusty Krab.

"Thanks for coming!" Mr. Krabs called after his defeated enemy. "Have a nice day!"

Outside, Plankton walked over to a signpost, leaned his forehead against it, and wept.

A little while later, Mr. Krabs watched Plankton through a telescope. He was still leaning against the signpost. "He's been out there crying for twenty minutes," Mr. Krabs said. "Pathetic." He peered through the telescope, then snapped it shut. "I'm just gonna go out there and gloat a little!"

Humming a happy tune, Mr. Krabs hurried out the front door.

Meanwhile, inside the safe in Mr. Krabs's office, Plankton's last penny was doing something unusual for a coin.

It was moving.

The penny wiggled, stood on edge, rolled, and

suddenly popped open. Hidden inside the penny was . . . PLANKTON!

He laughed and spoke into a tiny microphone hidden inside the penny. "Cyclops to Laptop," he said. "Cyclops to Laptop. Come in, Laptop!"

In the Chum Bucket, Plankton's computer wife, Karen, was playing solitaire on her screen. She heard her husband and answered, "Laptop? You DO realize that nickname is demeaning. I have TWICE the processing power of a laptop!"

Plankton answered in code. "Chicken is in the bread pan, kicking out dough."

But Karen didn't understand. "Wait," she said, confused. "You're in a bread pan?"

Annoyed that she'd forgotten their secret code, Plankton snapped, "Never mind. Maintain radio silence." He looked around the inside of Mr. Krabs's safe and spotted the Krabby Patty secret formula rolled up and corked in a bottle. "Finally!" he said, laughing triumphantly.

He was about to grab the bottle when he noticed it was sitting on a metal plate. "A pressure plate, eh, Krabs?" he said, snorting with contempt. "Amateur hour!"

Plankton opened the door to the safe and cautiously looked around Mr. Krabs's office. "Hm," he said. Then he saw a ship in a bottle on Mr. Krabs's desk. "Perfect!"

He yanked the miniature ship out of the bottle and tossed it in the trash. After finding a pad of paper and a pencil, he quickly scribbled a fake formula, tore out the page and rolled it up, then shoved it in the bottle. Plankton pushed the cork back in the bottle and admired his work.

"Not a bad likeness," he said with a smirk. "Good enough to fool that idiot Krabs!"

Back in the safe, Plankton carefully slid the fake formula bottle onto the pressure plate, simultaneously easing off the real bottle. "Easy . . . easy . . . ," he said as he worked. After a moment, he'd done it: the fake formula bottle was on the pressure plate, and the real formula bottle was in his dishonest hand!

In the dining area, SpongeBob was using the telescope to watch Mr. Krabs outside. His boss was gleefully dancing around the sobbing Plankton. "Look at Mr. Krabs go!" SpongeBob said. "I've never seen him gloat this hard before."

As he danced, Mr. Krabs sang a little song: *"Plankton's broke! Ooh! Ooh! Plankton's broke! Ah! Ah!"*

Mr. Krabs stopped dancing and laughed. "Well, Plankton, me bunions are tellin' me it's time to stop gloating." He picked up Plankton, who was still sobbing.

He noticed what looked like a loose thread. "Heh!" he said. "Looks like you're fallin' apart at the seams!"

When Mr. Krabs pulled on the thread, Plankton's skin unraveled, revealing metal underneath. It wasn't Plankton he was holding. It was a tiny Plankton robot!

"Huh?" Mr. Krabs said.

"Poor me," cried the robot. "Sob. . . . Sob. . . ."

"A ROBOT?" Mr. Krabs shouted.

Inside the Krusty Krab, SpongeBob walked into Mr. Krabs's office and saw . . . the open safe!

CHAPTER 5

SpongeBob gasped. "Plankton?"

Startled, Plankton whirled around, knocking the fake formula bottle off the pressure plate with the real formula bottle. An alarm sounded. *WHOOP! WHOOP! WHOOP!*

"Uh-oh," Plankton said. "That ain't good."

A computer voice came over a loudspeaker: "Initiating lockdown sequence."

Outside, Mr. Krabs heard the alarm go off. "Me formuler!" he cried, dropping the tiny Plankton robot.

As Mr. Krabs ran to the front door, the robot continued to whimper, "Poor me. . . . Sob. . . . Sob. . . ."

Inside the Krusty Krab, the lockdown sequence had begun. Metal shutters slammed down around every part of the restaurant. *SLAM! SLAM! SLAM!* The big sheets of metal surrounded Squidward's workstation.

"Huh?" Squidward said. Another metal shutter

slammed into place. "Ow," he said, trapped.

Metal shutters closed off the kitchen, the bathrooms, and even the customers' food so no one could possibly escape from the restaurant. Outside, Mr. Krabs watched a heavy metal shutter cover the front doors.

He ran as fast as he could, yelling, "Oh, no! OH, NO, NO, NO!" But he was too late. The last shutter closed. *SLAM!*

"NOOOOOO!" Mr. Krabs wailed. "Squidward! Can you hear me? Open up! SQUIDWARD!"

But Squidward was tightly enclosed in metal shutters. He couldn't get out of his little boat cash register station, let alone walk to the front door and somehow open it.

The Plankton robot picked itself up and started to dance. "Ha, ha. Victory dance," it gloated in its electronic voice.

Back in Mr. Krabs's office, SpongeBob and Plankton were struggling over the bottle that held the Krabby Patty secret formula.

"Gimme that!" SpongeBob panted.

"Come on, SpongeBob," Plankton urged. "Join me and we'll be rich and powerful . . . until I eventually betray you!" He realized what he'd said. "Uh, JOIN ME!"

SpongeBob shook his head violently. "No! NEVER! I'm on Team Krabs for life!"

Outside the front door, Mr. Krabs used all the strength he could muster to force the metal shutters open. He burst through the front door and called out, "PLANKTON!"

In the office, SpongeBob and Plankton were still trying to pull the formula bottle away from each other. They tugged. They strained. They yanked with all their might.

Suddenly, the bottle vanished into thin air!

SpongeBob's mouth hung open. He was completely flummoxed. "What? Where'd it go?" he asked.

"What?" Plankton said, equally confused. "Molecular deconstruction? But I proved that to be a scientific impossibility seven times!"

Mr. Krabs dashed in. He immediately saw that the safe was open and Plankton was standing there. The REAL Plankton—not a robot.

"Where's me formuler, Plankton?"

Plankton raised his tiny hands and shrugged. "I . . . I . . . I don't know. It just disappeared."

"Why should I believe YOU, you lyin' liar?" Mr. Krabs roared.

SpongeBob stepped forward. "Normally I'd agree with you, Mr. Krabs," he said. "But this time he's telling the truth! The formula just vanished . . . like magic!"

"It's true!" Plankton cried, nodding vigorously.

Mr. Krabs wasn't buying it. He grabbed Plankton and taped him to his desk. SpongeBob watched his boss, looking worried. "Mr. Krabs, I'm telling you," he insisted. "Plankton is innocent!"

"What are you going to do, Krabs?" Plankton asked, his voice trembling a little. "Pour hot oil on me? Put bamboo shoots under my nails?"

Mr. Krabs shook his head. "No," he said seriously. "Knock-knock."

Plankton grinned. "Knock-knock jokes?" he sneered. "I can do this all day, Krabs."

"Knock-knock," Mr. Krabs repeated.

"Oh, boy," Plankton said, smiling and rolling his eye. "Who's there?"

"Jimmy."

"Jimmy who?"

"Jimmy back my formuler, Plankton!" Mr. Krabs answered.

Plankton looked confused. "Well, that's stupid, but how is it torture?"

"You'll see," Mr. Krabs said, chuckling as he put on soundproof headphones.

SpongeBob was thinking hard. "Jimmy . . .

back . . . my . . . formula," he said to himself slowly. "Oh! I get it!" He started to laugh his high, annoying laugh. "DI YI YI YI YI YI YI!"

He kept laughing. And laughing. And laughing . . .

"MAKE IT STOP, KRABS!" Plankton screamed.

But Mr. Krabs just stood there wearing his headphones. And SpongeBob kept laughing. "DI YI YI YI YI YI YI YI YI!"

"OH, MAKE IT STOP, PLEASE!" Plankton shrieked.

"DI YI YI YI YI YI YI YI YI YI YI YI YI YI! DI YI YI YI YI YI YI . . ."

CHAPTER 6

As SpongeBob continued to laugh at the knock-knock joke, Squidward opened the door to the office. Behind him, a throng of angry customers scowled and complained.

"Mr. Krabs?" Squidward said. But Mr. Krabs couldn't hear him because of his headphones. And SpongeBob was still laughing as Plankton writhed in psychological pain.

"Zip it," Squidward commanded. SpongeBob immediately stopped laughing.

Plankton looked immensely relieved. "Oh, thank you, Squidward," he sighed.

Squidward ignored Plankton's apology. "The customers are getting restless," he said. "They're asking for . . . REFUNDS."

To Mr. Krabs, "refund" was such a horrible, terrifying word that he could hear it even through his soundproof headphones. "REFUNDS?" he said, gasping.

Sure enough, the customers were chanting "Re-fund. . . . Re-fund. . . . Re-fund" like a mob of zombies.

Mr. Krabs grabbed SpongeBob by his skinny arms. "Listen up, boy!" he cried. "Get in there and make me customers some Krabby Patties!" He hustled SpongeBob out of his office and shoved him through the kitchen door. Then he hurried back to his office.

"All right, Plankton . . . ," Mr. Krabs started to say. But when he looked at his desk, he saw that Plankton was GONE!

"Huh?" Mr. Krabs said. He had used his strongest tape to hold Plankton down.

"AAAAHHHH!" SpongeBob screamed from the kitchen. Mr. Krabs ran to see what was wrong. When he burst into the kitchen, he found his fry cook staring into the freezer.

"SpongeBob! What's wrong, boy?" Mr. Krabs asked. Then he looked into the freezer himself.

It was empty.

"WE'RE OUT OF KRABBY PATTIES?" Mr. Krabs screamed.

SpongeBob started to sweat despite the cold air pouring out of the freezer. "How can we make more Krabby Patties without the secret formula?"

Mr. Krabs paced around the kitchen, concentrating. "You've GOT to have that formuler memorized by now! You musta made a MILLION of those things!"

"But as you are aware, sir," SpongeBob reminded him, "the Employee Handbook clearly states, and I quote, 'No employee may in part, or in whole, commit the Krabby Patty secret formula to any recorded, written, or visual form, including memories, dreams, and/or needlepoint.'"

Mr. Krabs sobbed. "Oh, curse you, fine print!"

Out in the dining area, the crowd of hungry customers was still chanting. "Re-fund. . . . Re-fund. . . . Re-fund. . . ."

Mr. Krabs looked determined. "I've never given a refund in me life. And I'm not about to start TODAY!"

He burst into the dining room and told the angry mob that Plankton was the one who had taken the Krabby Patties away from them. SpongeBob tried to tell his boss that Plankton hadn't taken the secret formula, but Mr. Krabs ignored him. He led the furious customers out of the Krusty Krab and over to the Chum Bucket to get Plankton.

SpongeBob was left standing alone in the Krusty Krab. "But Plankton didn't do it," he said.

In the Chum Bucket, Plankton was telling Karen what had happened. "I had the secret formula right in my greedy little mitts, and then POOF! It just disappeared!"

The mob burst into his restaurant, led by Mr. Krabs. Mr. Krabs grabbed Plankton and carried him outside.

"All right, Plankton," Mr. Krabs said menacingly. "We'd like to have a word with you. . . ."

CHAPTER 7

Mr. Krabs roughly threw Plankton to the ground. Squidward, the starving customers, and Karen gathered around.

"Heh, heh," Plankton managed to chuckle. "You all look very hungry. Can I get anybody a Chum Burger?"

Mr. Krabs leaned over Plankton. "Enough with the niceties, Plankton," he snarled. "This is the last time I'm gonna ask you: Where is me formuler?"

Plankton tried to scoot away from his enemy. "I told you, Krabs! I don't have it!"

"Wrong answer," Mr. Krabs said, lifting his foot to stomp Plankton.

"STOP!" cried a voice.

Mr. Krabs hesitated and looked around. He saw his fry cook. And he looked mad.

"All right, Plankton," SpongeBob said with a growl. "I can't do my job without that formula. And when I can't do my job, I get mad. REAL mad!"

He kicked over a trash container. Then he quickly knelt down and cleaned up the garbage that had spilled all over the ground.

"Oh, sorry about that," he said. He held up an empty can. "You guys have a recycling bin for this? No? Okay, I'll just hang on to it and throw it away later." He put the can in his pocket and stood up.

"All right, Mr. Krabs," SpongeBob growled. "Let me get in on this!"

Plankton looked confused. "What's going on around here?" he asked.

SpongeBob walked over to Plankton, pushing up his short white sleeves. "You may wanna stand back a little, Mr. Krabs," he warned. "This could get messy."

"Let's hope so," Mr. Krabs said.

SpongeBob leaned over and shoved his face close to Plankton's. "So you won't talk, eh, Plankton?" Plankton blinked. "I didn't wanna have to do this . . . ," SpongeBob said.

He pulled out a bottle of bubble solution, unscrewed the cap, and removed the wand. Then he expertly dipped the wand in the soapy liquid.

"Here comes the pain," SpongeBob said.

"Soap in the eye, eh?" Mr. Krabs said approvingly. "Diabolical."

SpongeBob took a deep breath and pursed his lips. Plankton held up his tiny hands.

"No!" Plankton cried. "Stop! Don't—"

SpongeBob blew a large, shiny bubble that surrounded Plankton completely. Mr. Krabs looked puzzled. "Wait," he said. "That doesn't look painful."

SpongeBob turned to Mr. Krabs. "Mr. Krabs," he explained. "You may not understand what I'm about to do today, but someday we'll look back"—he jumped inside the bubble with Plankton—"and have a good laugh."

As Mr. Krabs and the angry mob watched in disbelief, SpongeBob and Plankton floated up into the sky in their bubble.

"Hey!" cried one of the angry customers. "They're getting away!"

"Sorry, Mr. Krabs!" SpongeBob called down from the rising bubble.

Mr. Krabs shook his fist up at SpongeBob. "So you've been runnin' the long con on me, eh? All these years you've been workin' for PLANKTON!"

"They're in CAHOOTS!" shouted an angry customer.

"Yeah, I guess that's the short way of saying it," Mr. Krabs admitted. Then he jabbed his claw up toward the floating bubble. "STOP THAT BUBBLE!"

He and the mob ran after the bubble on the ground. They even launched one customer at the bubble. He hit it and held on for dear life.

"Please tell me there's something soft under me," he said to SpongeBob and Plankton.

"Um . . . nope," they answered.

He fell off, screaming.

"SPONGEBOB!" Mr. Krabs shouted as he watched the bubble disappear into the distance. "You were like an underpaid son to me! I would've expected Squidward to stab me in the back . . ."

At the sound of his name, Squidward woke from a brief snooze. "Huh? What? Huh?" he mumbled.

". . . but SpongeBob?" Mr. Krabs continued. "Me most trusted employee?" He took a deep breath. "You know what this means, Mr. Squidward?"

"We get the rest of the day off?" Squidward asked hopefully.

"No," Mr. Krabs said, shaking his head. "This be but a harbinger of what I fear lies ahead. For you, for me, for all of Bikini Bottom. The Krabby Patty is what ties us all together, and without it, there will be a complete breakdown of social order! A war of all against all! Dark times are ahead! Dark times indeed!"

Squidward scrunched up his face. "Seriously?" he asked. "Aren't you overreacting a bit?"

But when he looked around, Squidward saw that Bikini Bottom had already erupted into flames. People were looting stores and fighting each other over scraps of food. The town had become a violent, ugly place. And Squidward and Mr. Krabs themselves were suddenly wearing leather outfits that made them look tough.

"Welcome to the apocalypse, Mr. Squidward," Mr. Krabs said dramatically. "I hope you like leather."

"I prefer suede," Squidward said.

CHAPTER 8

Surrounded by attentive seagulls, Burger Beard read from the old book he'd stolen. He held it open to a picture of Bikini Bottom in flames. "'And so,'" he said. "'Bikini Bottom became an apocalyptic cesspool forevermore.'"

He snapped the book shut. "The end."

The seagulls were very upset. "What?" they cried. "No! The book has more pages than that!"

Humming and singing to himself, Burger Beard strolled over to the ship's wheel and steered.

A seagull landed on the wheel and said, "There is NO WAY that's the end of the story!"

"Well, of course it is!" Burger Beard insisted. "I'll show you. Turn around."

The seagull turned, and Burger Beard plucked a feather from its tail. "Hey!" the seagull cried. "I need that to fly, you jerk!"

Burger Beard dipped the point of the feather in black ink and wrote THE END in his book. Not wanting the story to end, one of the seagulls tried to pull the book out of his hands.

"Gimme that book!" the seagull squawked. He accidentally tore loose the page that Burger Beard had written on.

"HEY!" Burger Beard shouted. "Let go of that!"

The pirate scrambled to grab back the torn page, but he slipped and fell on the deck. *KLUNK!*

The seagull flapped its wings and flew off the ship with the page in its beak. Then it dropped the sheet into the water. "I shouldn't be littering," the seagull admitted, "but that ending was GARBAGE!"

Burger Beard jumped to his feet and started swatting at the seagulls. "Why, you sky scum!"

The page with THE END on it slowly sank into the briny depths. . . .

In Bikini Bottom, things had gone from bad to worse. Chaos reigned everywhere. Lawlessness ruled the streets. Fires, robbery, people bumping into each other without saying "Excuse me"—you name it.

Somehow Patrick didn't notice. He strolled into the Krusty Krab and cheerfully said, "Good morning, Squidward! I'll have the usual . . . with cheese."

Squidward shook his head. He couldn't believe Patrick hadn't heard the news. "We're out of Krabby Patties right now."

"Out of Krabby Patties?" Patrick said, surprised. "Okay, then, just gimme a double Krabby Patty."

Mr. Krabs ran out of the kitchen, waving his claws in the air. Flames shot out of the kitchen door. "Patrick!" he shouted. "THERE ARE NO KRABBY PATTIES!"

"No Krabby Patties? NOOOOOOOO!" he wailed.

SpongeBob peered through the bubble as it flew over his hometown. "Look what's become of Bikini Bottom!" he cried. "We really need to get that formula back!"

"Hmm," Plankton mused. "Get the secret formula, you say? Excuse me. I need a moment."

He turned away from SpongeBob and talked to himself. "With that formula, I could rule the

WORLD!" He muffled his evil laughter as best he could. Then he turned back to SpongeBob.

"Well, what do we do now?" Plankton asked innocently.

"Now we work TOGETHER!" he exclaimed. "You know, TEAMWORK!"

Plankton looked as though he had absolutely no idea what SpongeBob was talking about.

"What's a *tee-am* work?" he asked.

"No, Plankton," SpongeBob gently corrected him. "TEAMwork."

"*Tee-am* work," Plankton said.

"Teamwork."

"Tie 'em work."

"Teamwork."

"Tie 'em up."

SpongeBob sighed. "Say 'team,' like a sports . . ."

"Team," Plankton said.

"Team! Now say 'work.'"

"Work."

"Put 'em together and whaddya got?" SpongeBob asked hopefully.

"Time bomb," Plankton said. "Work."

"Gettin' better!" SpongeBob said encouragingly.

CHAPTER 9

Inside her treedome, Sandy sat down to watch TV and eat a Krabby Patty she'd been saving. "Mm-MMM!" she said, licking her lips. An anchorman came on the screen and announced, "Now: Bikini Bottom Action News!"

Sandy heard a strange noise above her. She looked up and saw Patrick stuck to the outside of her treedome, staring at her Krabby Patty and drooling.

"Oh!" Sandy said. "Uh, hey, Patrick!"

With his tongue stuck to the dome's glass, Patrick said, "KABBY! PABBY!"

When Sandy started to take a bite, Patrick pulled his tongue off the glass and said angrily, "KRABBY! PATTY!" He pounded the glass with his fists. "KRABBY! PATTY!"

Each time Sandy tried to take a bite of her sandwich, Patrick screamed, "KRABBY! PATTY!" Finally, she shoved the whole Krabby Patty into her mouth at once. Patrick screamed, slid off the glass, and wandered away miserably. "C'mon, tummy," he said sadly. "It's gonna be a long day."

Sandy watched him go. "What's gotten into Patrick?"

On the TV, the anchorman said urgently, "We interrupt your regular program for an important news bulletin!"

Reporter Perch Perkins appeared on the screen holding a microphone. "Perch Perkins, reporting live from downtown Bikini Bottom," he said, ducking as a boatmobile flew by his head.

"Complete chaos here today as our town attempts to deal with a sudden and complete shortage of Krabby Patties," he reported, ducking again to avoid a metal trash can. "Events here have this reporter wondering—what IS the secret ingredient in Krabby Patties, anyway?"

An angry fish ran up, waving a metal pipe. "It's love!" he yelled. "The secret ingredient is LOVE!"

Perch Perkins ran away screaming. The angry fish swung his pipe at the camera, and Sandy's TV screen went blank.

"No more Krabby Patties?" she said.

Suddenly, the inside of the treedome went dark. Sandy looked up and saw a huge shadow covering the curved glass. "Huh?" she said. "What the corn dog is THAT?"

The page from Burger Beard's book with THE END written on it had drifted down and landed on Sandy's treedome.

Up in their bubble, SpongeBob was still trying to teach Plankton about teamwork. "Come on, Plankton! It's easy! It means I help you, you help me, and when we accomplish our goal, we do 'hands in the middle'!"

"Hands in the middle?" Plankton said doubtfully. "No, no. Sounds idiotic." He looked down through the bubble to the town below. "Besides," he added, "the two of us are no match for that cranky mob!"

Down in Bikini Bottom, the angry horde was destroying a doughnut shop. They pushed on the side of the building until it tipped over and burst into flames. Doughnuts flew everywhere. People from the mob frantically gathered up doughnuts and carried them off, laughing hysterically, madness in their eyes.

"We could probably use a few more *tee-am* works," Plankton suggested.

SpongeBob brightened. "That's exactly what I was thinking!" He pulled a pin out of his pocket.

"Wait!" Plankton said, holding up both hands. "What are you doing?"

SpongeBob jammed the pin into the bubble. *POP!* He and Plankton plummeted through the air with Plankton screaming all the way!

*W*HUMP! SpongeBob and Plankton landed right next to Squidward's house. Plankton groaned, lying on the ground. SpongeBob quickly got to his feet and looked around.

What he saw surprised him.

Patrick was sitting on top of his house, banging his face against the rock. But instead of his usual shorts, he was wearing a futuristic-looking leather outfit.

Between face-bangs he said, "I. Need. Krabby Patties. I! Need! Krabby Patties!"

"Patrick!" SpongeBob yelled. "What are you doing?!"

Patrick stopped banging his face against his house and looked over at SpongeBob and Plankton. "Vandalizing stuff," he answered.

"But isn't that YOUR house?" Plankton asked.

"Hey!" Patrick snapped. "What's with all the questions? Who ARE you guys?"

SpongeBob couldn't believe Patrick had asked. They hadn't been up in the bubble that long. What was wrong with Patrick?

"It's me!" SpongeBob cried. "Your best friend! SpongeBob!"

Patrick looked skeptical. "Oh, yeah? Well, if you're SpongeBob, then what's the secret password?"

At the same time, SpongeBob and Plankton said, "Uh . . ."

"Correct!" Patrick declared with a nod. "It IS you! SPONGEBOB!"

Patrick jumped off his rock and landed on SpongeBob. *BLOMP!*

"SpongeBob!"

"Patrick!"

"SpongeBob, why aren't you at the Krusty Krab making Krabby Patties?"

Patrick sat down, right on top of Plankton.

"Well, I'd love to, but the formula is gone. We're putting together a team to get it back," SpongeBob explained.

"A team?" Patrick asked. "Ooh! Ooh! Pick me! Pick me!"

Patrick jumped up to give SpongeBob a big bear hug. Grinning, SpongeBob said, "Okay, Patrick! You're in!"

Plankton popped out of the sand. "I don't know, SpongeBob. What exactly does this clown bring to the *tee-am*?"

"He brings loyalty, Plankton." SpongeBob turned to his best friend. "Isn't that right, Patrick?"

Patrick said, "Yeah, yeah . . . loyalty." Then he suddenly yelled, "HE'S OVER HERE!" and started making alarm sounds. "WHOOP! WHOOP! WHOOP!"

SpongeBob pleaded with his buddy, "Patrick, I'm fleeing an angry mob right now, and this isn't helping!"

But it was too late. Mr. Krabs had already heard Patrick's alarm. "Let's go GET HIM!" he shouted to the furious, hungry customers.

Plankton started to run. "Come on, SpongeBob! Let's get out of here!"

"Patrick, please!" SpongeBob begged.

Patrick threw SpongeBob right on top of Plankton and then sat on them both, still making alarm sounds. "WHOOP! WHOOP! WHOOP!"

"Patrick!" SpongeBob cried. "Why are you doing this?"

"Because I. Need. KRABBY PATTIES!" Patrick said. He turned toward Mr. Krabs and the angry mob, who were running straight toward them. "Hurry up!" he shouted. "I'M HUNGRY! OVER HERE!"

Frantic to escape from his hunger-crazed friend, SpongeBob began furiously burrowing underground. Carrying Plankton in his hand, he tunneled away from Patrick. Then he popped up out of the ground, gasping and panting.

As the mob grew closer, SpongeBob and Plankton ran away as fast as their legs could carry them. Patrick called, "Guys? Am I still on the team?"

Plankton grumbled, "Well, your stupid friend gave us away. So who's the NEXT member of our *tee-am*?"

SpongeBob thought for a minute. "I know! Sandy! She's smart!"

The two fugitives ran straight to Sandy's treedome. SpongeBob opened the air-lock door, rushed inside, and slammed the door shut. He put on a water helmet and pressed a big red button. The water in the air lock drained. SpongeBob scooped Plankton into a glass of water before he dried out.

"Sandy?" SpongeBob called.

They opened the second air lock and stepped inside the dome. It was dark and eerie. Pieces of paper were stuck all over the inside of the dome, blocking the light. "Sandy?" SpongeBob repeated.

They walked farther inside but didn't find Sandy

anywhere. "Sandy? Are you home?" SpongeBob called. He turned to Plankton. "Gee, I wonder where she is!"

The two of them looked more closely at the papers stuck to the inside of the dome. They were covered with scribbles and strange writing, all connected by string. "What IS this stuff?" SpongeBob asked.

As they stared at the papers, a dark shape whipped by, passing right behind them. SpongeBob turned around.

"Sandy?" he asked. "Is that you?"

CHAPTER 11

SpongeBob reached toward one of the papers and a hand grabbed his shoulder.

"Hey!" Sandy said sharply. "Don't touch those papers!"

Sandy darted away and picked up a thick notebook. She opened it and started reading, mumbling to herself. "'Krabby Patties . . . chaos . . . secret ingredient . . .'" SpongeBob and Plankton slowly walked over to her.

She didn't seem like the old Sandy SpongeBob knew and loved.

"Sandy," he asked, "are you okay?"

She wheeled around and stared at him. "'Okay?' Have you looked outside?" Sandy pointed out the glass wall of her treedome to Bikini Bottom, where they could see flames and plumes of black smoke. "Does that seem okay to you?" she demanded.

Sandy started pacing. "I'm trying to figure out

what happened to society. If we don't fix it soon, there won't be anything left to fix!" She twitched, and her eyes bulged out of her head.

"Lack of Krabby Patties has driven her mad!" SpongeBob whispered to Plankton.

Sandy stared at the papers stuck inside her treedome. She grabbed her head with her hands. "I think I figured it out! LOOK!"

She grabbed some papers and tore them off the curved glass dome. Through the dome, SpongeBob and Plankton could see a big sheet of paper with THE END on it.

Sandy stabbed her finger at the big sheet of paper. "When this came down from above, I knew it could only mean one thing. ONLY ONE THING!"

SpongeBob looked puzzled. "And that would be . . . ?"

Sandy whipped around and held her hands wide apart. "It MEANS it's THE END!"

"I see," Plankton said from his glass of water, humoring her. "That certainly clears that up."

"And I know why it's the end," Sandy continued. "The SANDWICH GODS are ANGRY with us!"

Now SpongeBob and Plankton were really confused. "Sandwich gods?" they asked.

Sandy started pacing again, moving even faster

this time, waving her hands through the air. "I just don't know how we're going to APPEASE them!"

"Well, maybe you should sacrifice an innocent," Plankton said sarcastically. "Then Krabby Patties will rain down from the sky. That always works!"

Plankton realized that while he'd been making this sarcastic suggestion, he had risen up above the water level in his glass. "Excuse me," he said, and dove back under the water.

Sandy thought about Plankton's idea. "A sacrifice?" she mused. "That makes PERFECT sense!"

She ran around her treedome, feverishly scribbling on the pieces of paper stuck to the inside of the glass. "'Sacrifice . . . innocent . . . sandwich gods . . . ,'" she muttered as she wrote.

SpongeBob and Plankton slowly backed away from Sandy and then hurried through the air lock to get away from the deranged squirrel.

Outside, Plankton said, "Well, THAT was a complete waste of time. . . ."

Inside the cabin of his ship, Burger Beard lay in bed, reading from the old book. Seagulls were tucked in next to him.

"That's all for now," he said, closing the book dramatically. "You sleepy little birds get some rest. We can finish in the morning."

Kyle looked up at him with his big brown eyes. "Pwease," he pleaded. "Just one more stowy, Mistew Piwate! Pwease?"

Burger Beard tried to resist the adorable little seagull but failed. "Oh, all right, Kyle," he relented. "How can I say no to you? One more story . . ."

"Yay!" Kyle cheered. "We WUV a good stowy! But nothing too scawy, Mistew Piwate!"

Burger Beard climbed out of bed and picked up a candle. The yellow light flickered below his face. "How about THIS story? There once was a pirate who dreamed of being the world's greatest galley chef. . . ."

He held the candle close to an old picture in a frame. It showed Burger Beard when he was young, cooking behind a grill crowded with food.

"They all laughed at him in pirate school," he continued. "But with the help of this magical book"—he held up the old book he'd stolen—"he would SHOW them! He would show them ALL!"

Burger Beard grinned a horrible grin in the candlelight.

"But, Mistew Piwate," Kyle asked innocently, "what makes that book so magical?"

"I'll show you," the pirate answered. He quickly scribbled in the book, and suddenly the seagulls were wearing pirate hats and eye patches! Cackling, Burger Beard told them, "Now say 'Ahhhhrrrr!'"

"Ahhhhrrrr!" said the seagulls.

Burger Beard laughed and blew out the candle.

CHAPTER 12

When SpongeBob saw his pineapple home, he gasped. It had been severely damaged by a wandering mob! And for some reason, it was covered in gooey snail slime.

Where was SpongeBob's beloved pet snail?

"Gare-bear?" SpongeBob called.

A blob of snail slime dripped onto SpongeBob's head. "Revolting!" Plankton said.

"But it means Gary is close by!" SpongeBob observed, ever hopeful. "Gary! I'm back!"

When they walked into the broken house, they suddenly stopped, shocked by what they saw.

"Whoa," SpongeBob said.

The house was filled with snails. Big snails. Small snails. Snails of every color and description. And they were all looking respectfully at . . .

Gary. SpongeBob's pet snail was sitting on a giant throne, surrounded by pillars and huge fire pits.

"Oh, hey, Gary!" SpongeBob exclaimed happily. "Plankton and I need you to help us find the Krabby Patty formula and fix Bikini Bottom!"

"Meow!" Gary said.

"What do you mean, you don't have to do as I say anymore?"

"Meow!"

"What do you mean, King of the Snails?" Looking stern, SpongeBob folded his arms. "Gary the snail, you get down here RIGHT NOW and join this team!"

"Meow!"

"What do you mean, 'Seize them!'?"

All the snails who had been paying their respects to Gary, the King of the Snails, turned to SpongeBob and Plankton. Then they advanced on them with their fangs bared, growling!

SpongeBob turned and ran out of the pineapple house as fast as he could!

"Why are you running?" Plankton asked.

"Because they're right on our ... ." He looked back to see the snails moving very, very slowly.

"Oh, right," SpongeBob said, slowing his pace. "Snails."

The two unlikely partners strolled away from SpongeBob's house. "Well, so much for your *tee-am*," Plankton said.

"Putting together a team is a LOT harder than I thought it would be!" SpongeBob admitted.

Nearby, Mr. Krabs shouted, "This way!" The angry mob was still on their tail.

"We better get out of here until things cool off," Plankton said.

That night, high on a ridge overlooking Bikini Bottom, Plankton and SpongeBob looked down at their hometown. They could see fires burning in the darkness.

"Everything we know and love has been destroyed!" SpongeBob said sadly.

"Looks like they're gonna have to change the name of Bikini Bottom to Dirty Bottom," Plankton said, chuckling. "Right, SpongeBob?"

SpongeBob wrinkled his nose and frowned. "That's a little gross, Plankton."

"Yeah," Plankton said. "Yeah. Too soon, huh?"

SpongeBob stared into distance. "This feels like it really IS the end!"

"Don't worry, SpongeBob," Plankton reassured him. "We'll find the secret formula, and everything will go back to the way it was. You know, all happy and junk."

He pushed a rock toward SpongeBob. "Now let's try to get some sleep."

"Yeah, I guess you're right," SpongeBob said, laying his head on the rock.

Plankton pulled a blanket of seaweed over Sponge-Bob. "There you are," he said. "Feeling comfy?"

"You know, Plankton," SpongeBob said sleepily, "I think you might know a little bit more about teamwork than you let on."

"Good night, SpongeBob."

"Good night, Plankton."

Exhausted from the day, SpongeBob instantly fell into a deep sleep.

Plankton let out an evil little chuckle. "Good night indeed!" he said to himself. He crept up onto SpongeBob's head. "That's right, SpongeBob, sleep! You're hiding that formula in there somewhere. . . ."

Plankton forced one of SpongeBob's holes open and jumped into his head!

CHAPTER 13

Once inside SpongeBob's head, Plankton wasted no time going straight to his brain, hoping to find the Krabby Patty secret formula. "Well," he said. "Here goes nothing!"

The inside of SpongeBob's brain was colorful and bright, with funny shapes and happy music. "Huh?" Plankton said. "What IS this place?"

A bottle of maple syrup ran by laughing, chased by a waffle, which was also laughing. "Hee hee! I'm gonna get you!" said the waffle.

Plankton was confused.

Two ice cream cones threw fudge at each other. "Fudge fight!" they said, laughing.

"Hmm," Plankton said. "Apparently it's very sweet inside SpongeBob's brain. After talking to SpongeBob, I thought it'd be mostly empty. But that secret formula's got to be in here somewhere. . . ."

As he started to search through SpongeBob's brain, Plankton heard two voices calling to him. "Hello, Plankton! Come play with us!"

He turned and saw two ice pops stuck together. They were smiling at him. "Hurry!" they called. "Before we MELT!" They giggled.

Horrified, Plankton ran away, scattering a bunch of happy balloons. He passed a doughnut blowing bubbles out of its hole. Screaming, Plankton ran off the edge of a cliff, landing in a pile of cute little fur balls!

The fur balls pushed together and transformed into a single giant kitten. It was cute but gigantic. Looming over Plankton, the kitten purred and meowed.

"So . . . much . . . sweetness," Plankton groaned, heaving. "I think I'm going to be sick."

He threw up, but what came out of his mouth was a giant rainbow! He stared at the rainbow in disbelief. The giant rainbow suddenly grew arms and eyes.

"DADDY!" cried the giant rainbow.

Plankton screamed and ran away again. Soon he popped out of SpongeBob's ear and landed next to their cold campfire. His grunts and groans awakened SpongeBob.

"Plankton?" he asked groggily. "Plankton! I just had the craziest dream, and you were in it!"

Plankton was covered in cotton candy, cookie crumbs, and caramel sauce. "I'm sure it was nothing," he said quickly. "Now go back to sleep."

"Well, good night," SpongeBob said. But as he lay down, he noticed a candy cane stuck to Plankton's head.

"Were you in my brain?" SpongeBob asked.

"What? No," Plankton insisted. "That's crazy talk."

"Then why is there cotton candy on your antennae?"

"Because . . . um . . . ," Plankton said, stumped. "Okay, fine! I was in your brain!"

SpongeBob gasped, stepped back, and covered his head with his hands. "What were you doing in there?"

Plankton rolled his eye. "What do you THINK I was doing? Looking for the secret formula."

"WHAT?" SpongeBob cried.

"Don't act so innocent!" Plankton sneered. "You knew what I was up to. That's why you're pretending not to know the formula!"

SpongeBob looked shocked. "I'm not pretending! I can't believe you thought I was lying!"

Plankton shrugged. "Hey, don't take it personally. I just assume everyone's lying."

"That is a horrible way to live your life."

"Whatever," Plankton said.

"It is! And if we're going to be on the same team—"

Plankton jumped to his feet and shook his fist. "Maybe I don't want to be on a *tee-am*! You ever think of that?"

"But, Plankton," SpongeBob protested. "EVERYTHING's better when you're part of a team!" With that, he pulled out a pitch pipe and blew through it.

"You're not going to start singing, are you?" Plankton asked, shaking his head.

But he was. SpongeBob sang a song about teamwork—about how nothing is impossible if you tackle it as a team. In his enthusiasm, SpongeBob picked up Plankton during the song. After the song was over, Plankton said, "All right, you can put me down."

SpongeBob gently set Plankton on the ground. "Well, that's one minute of my life I'll never get back," Plankton complained.

"Not without a time machine," SpongeBob pointed out.

Plankton froze. "Wait a minute!" he said. "Repeat that! Slowly!"

"Not . . . without . . . a . . . time . . . machine," SpongeBob said in a slow, deep voice.

"Yes!" Plankton shouted. "THAT'S IT!"

CHAPTER 14

"SpongeBob, you're a genius!" Plankton cried, clapping him on the back.

"I am?" SpongeBob asked, puzzled.

"If we build a time machine," Plankton explained enthusiastically, "we can go back to before the formula disappeared! Before society broke down! Before we became the hunted!"

SpongeBob looked doubtful. "That sounds great, Plankton," he said. "But how do we build a time machine?"

Plankton paced back and forth, thinking. "Well," he said slowly, "first we'll need a computer powerful enough to calculate the intricacies of time travel."

"Where would we get one of those?" SpongeBob asked.

"I just happen to be married to one," Plankton answered with a smile.

INVINCIBUBBLE

WITH HIS POWERFUL
BUBBLE BLOWER,
HE CAN TRAP
ANYTHING
HE AIMS AT
AND MAKE IT
HARMLESSLY
FLOAT AWAY!

MR. SUPER-AWESOMENESS

THIS PINK
MENACE HAS
TELEKINETIC
POWERS THAT
ENABLE HIM
TO CONTROL
ANYTHING
MADE OF
ICE CREAM.

SOUR NOTE

HE HAS A POWERFUL TELESCOPING CLARINET THAT BLASTS THE MOST OBNOXIOUS NOTE EVER PLAYED, SENDING CROWDS RUNNING FOR COVER!

THE RODENT

SHE'S A GIANT
REALISTIC
SQUIRREL
WITH THE
ABILITY TO DO
SUPER-SQUIRREL
THINGS, LIKE SPIT
OUT CHEEKFULS
OF ROASTED NUTS!

SIR PINCH-A-LOT

THIS SUPER CRUSTACEAN HAS GIANT CLAWS THAT SHOOT LIKE ROCKETS, AND HE CAN TRANSFORM HIMSELF INTO A JET-POWERED FLYING CRAB.

HE HAS THE BODY OF A MEGA-MUSCLEMAN AND THE STRENGTH TO MATCH! TOO BAD HIS HEAD STAYED THE SAME OLD SIZE.
PLANK-TON

High on another cliff at the edge of Bikini Bottom, SpongeBob and Plankton looked down at the Chum Bucket. It was surrounded by guards. And they looked angry.

"Those thugs have got Karen tied up in the back room," Plankton said. "We're going to have to sneak by them. You know, it's funny. I've never seen this many people at the Chum Bucket."

"I know!" SpongeBob exclaimed. "I've never seen ANYONE there."

Plankton looked exasperated. "Now, was that really necessary?"

"Because the food's really bad."

"Oh, come on! REALLY?"

"SHH!" SpongeBob said. "How are we gonna sneak past those guards?"

"Hmm . . . ," Plankton said, thinking of a plan.

Moments later, a tire rolled down the cliff toward the Chum Bucket. When it reached the bottom of the cliff, it kept going, rolling right into the middle of a group of guards.

"Well, what do we have here?" asked one guard.

The guards pulled out some wooden sticks and metal rods and started beating the tire!

Behind them, SpongeBob and Plankton sneaked over to the Chum Bucket, hidden in a stack of tires. "We'd better hurry," SpongeBob whispered. "Those guys really hate tires!"

Plankton tried to open a small door, but it was locked. "We'll never get in!" he cried. "The door's locked!"

"A team doesn't give up that easily," SpongeBob reassured him. "Let me take a closer look."

SpongeBob climbed out of the stack of tires and examined the side of the Chum Bucket more carefully. When he looked up, he saw an open window.

"There!" he said. "That window's open! C'mon, Plankton. Time for some real teamwork. Gimme a boost."

"Okay . . . ," Plankton said uncertainly. Then he saw SpongeBob's shiny black shoe coming down at him. "Wait a minute! NO!"

Plankton tried with all his might to hold up SpongeBob by his shoe, but he just didn't have enough strength. *SQUISH!*

Not realizing what had happened, Sponge-Bob was still straining to reach the open window.

"Just . . . a . . . little . . . higher, Plankton," he said. Then he realized Plankton wasn't answering him. "Plankton?"

When SpongeBob lifted his shoe and looked at its sole, he saw Plankton flattened across it.

"Why don't YOU boost ME up instead?" Plankton suggested sensibly.

"Oh, yeah," SpongeBob said. "Good thinking!"

SpongeBob lifted his shoe up to the open window and scraped Plankton off. Groaning, Plankton landed on the windowsill. Then he jumped through the window into the Chum Bucket. As soon as he hit the floor, he ran to the small door and opened it.

"Come on, SpongeBob!" he whispered intensely. "Come on!"

SpongeBob squeezed through the small door and into the restaurant. "We're in!" he said. Then he swung the door closed. *SLAM!*

"Shhhh!" Plankton hissed. "There's a guard over there!"

Plankton pointed across the room at the guard. It was Patrick, snoring loudly as he slept in a chair by another door. "The key's around his neck!" Plankton whispered. "We can take it from him, but we'll have to be very quiet. Let's walk on the tips of our toes."

Plankton raised himself up on the tips of his

toes—which SpongeBob had never noticed before—and skittered across the floor. There was a high, tinkling sound.

Patrick stirred in his sleep. Plankton froze, but the high tinkling sound continued. He looked back and saw SpongeBob playing a tiny piano. "Will you stop playing that tiny piano?" he said. "You're going to get us caught!"

SpongeBob sheepishly put the tiny piano away. "Sorry," he apologized.

They both tiptoed over to Patrick, who was still snoring. The key was on his chest, hanging on a chain around his neck.

"Okay," Plankton said to SpongeBob. "Just reach out and grab that key!"

SpongeBob took a step closer to Patrick and stepped on a floorboard. *CREAK!*

"Halt!" Patrick said sleepily. "Who goes there?" But then he fell right back to sleep. *ZZZZZZZZZZZZZ!*

SpongeBob gently grabbed the key and pulled it down.

"Stop!" Plankton hissed. "Pull it over his head!"

"Oh," SpongeBob said. He lifted the key up toward Patrick's head, but the chain got caught in the folds of Patrick's neck fat.

"Stop! STOP!" Plankton warned. SpongeBob

let go of the key. "Let me get up there," Plankton continued. "I'm smaller. I won't wake him up."

Plankton jumped onto Patrick and climbed up to the key. He yanked the chain free, but then the key slid down Patrick's chest, heading straight for his belly button. Plankton leapt onto the key and rode it like a snowboard.

"YAAAAHHH!" he screamed as he headed into Patrick's belly button. Just as he and the key were about to completely disappear into the depths of Patrick's navel, SpongeBob plucked them out, covered in gross lint.

They had the key! Success!

Except—at that very moment, Patrick woke up.

When he saw SpongeBob and Patrick, he pulled out a giant whistle and inhaled, ready to blow a mighty blast!

"NO!" SpongeBob yelled, tackling Patrick. The two buddies struggled. Patrick kept trying to put his lips on the whistle, but SpongeBob kept stopping him.

"Plankton, help!" SpongeBob shouted. "I'll rock him, and you tell him a bedtime story!"

SpongeBob flipped Patrick over onto his lap. Plankton jumped onto Patrick's belly and talked quickly. "Once upon a time there was a big fat pink idiot who went to sleep. The end!"

"Nice try," Patrick scoffed, "but it's gonna take more than that to—"

And he fell fast asleep.

SpongeBob and Plankton lost no time using the key to open the door. They burst through to find . . .

CHAPTER 15

○ ○ ○ **K**aren chained to the wall!

"I told you I don't have the formula, you monsters!" cried Plankton's computer wife.

"Hey, baby!" Plankton called. "How are you?"

Karen was thrilled to see her husband. "Plankton! My hero!" She stopped. "You must need something. Otherwise, you wouldn't have come back."

"Plankton has a plan to save Bikini Bottom!" SpongeBob said as he unlocked Karen's chains.

If Karen could have shaken her head, she would have. "It's impossible, Sheldon," she said. "Krabs knows all your plans. He's been through my hard drive looking for the secret formula."

Plankton hung his head. "Eh, I never had it." Then he looked up and smiled. "But we're gonna get it! We're going back in time to steal the formula before it disappeared!"

"Really? Time travel?" Karen asked incredulously.

"Where are you going to find a computer that can do THAT?"

Instantly, her powerful computer brain gave her the answer. "Wait a minute . . . ," she said.

Outside, SpongeBob and Plankton sneaked away from the Chum Bucket carrying Karen's head. "I've never carried a head before," SpongeBob whispered.

"You'll get used to it," Plankton said.

"It's still warm," SpongeBob said in a little voice.

They left the angry guards behind, still beating the tire. "So you won't talk, eh?" one of the guards snarled. "Let some air out of him!"

At an abandoned Mexican-German restaurant called Taco Haüs, SpongeBob carefully set Karen's head on the floor. "Is this where we're going to build our time machine?" he asked, looking around at the dusty restaurant.

Plankton nodded. "Sure! It's got everything we need! A photo booth, a cuckoo clock, some stale chips. . . . Now all we have to do is build it!"

Seeing another opportunity for a song about teamwork, SpongeBob happily pulled out his trusty pitch pipe and blew into it.

"Oh, no, you don't!" Plankton protested.

"Hey!" SpongeBob cried.

"I, uh, need it," Plankton said. "For, um . . . the time machine!"

"Oh, okay!"

Plankton took the pitch pipe into another room. *WHAM! WHAM! WHAM! WHAM!* It sounded as though he was smashing something with a hammer. *FLUSH!* Then it sounded like he was flushing something down a toilet. "Installed!" he announced when he came back.

And so, working together, along with Karen's powerful brain, using the crummy materials they found in the abandoned restaurant, Plankton and SpongeBob built a time machine. When they were done, Plankton spun the hands on the cuckoo clock, and an engine roared to life. *VRROOM!*

"I did it!" Plankton said proudly.

"No, WE did it!" SpongeBob corrected him.

"We DID do it," Plankton admitted, "as a *tee-am*!"

"A TEAM!" SpongeBob said.

"Whatever," Plankton said, climbing into the photo booth. "Say 'Cheese!'"

"Cheese!"

The time machine sputtered and died.

Plankton stepped out of the booth. "What's WRONG with this thing?" he fumed, studying his time-machine blueprint. "I don't understand! We got EVERYTHING! It makes no SENSE!"

"Sense?" SpongeBob mused. "Cents!" He pulled a quarter out of his pocket. "Twenty-five cents, to be exact!"

SpongeBob dropped the quarter in the photo booth's slot, and the time machine started right back up. *VRROOM! WHIRRRR!*

SpongeBob and Plankton jumped into the time machine. "So," SpongeBob said, looking around, "how do we tell this time machine where to go?"

"I don't know," Plankton said. "Let's try THIS button!"

He pressed a big green button. Lights flashed! SpongeBob and Plankton hurtled back through time. When they stopped, SpongeBob cautiously slid open the photo booth's curtain and stepped out.

The time machine was sitting in the middle of a desolate wasteland. There was no sign of Bikini Bottom anywhere.

"According to my calculations, the Krusty Krab should be right here," Plankton said, puzzled.

SpongeBob pointed. "What's that over there?"

He ran over and found Patrick! But Patrick was much, much older, with a long beard.

"Patrick?" SpongeBob asked.

"SpongeBob?" older Patrick croaked. "Is it really you?"

"Yes, Patrick, it's—"

"Finally, the Great Krabby Patty Famine is OVER!" Patrick cried in gratitude.

"Great Krabby Patty Famine?" SpongeBob said. "What year IS this?"

"It's Thursday," Patrick answered.

"According to my calculations, we've only gone four days into the future," Plankton explained.

Patrick was celebrating. "They said you'd never come back, but I knew you would!"

"Where's the Krusty Krab?" SpongeBob asked, looking around.

Patrick shrugged. "Same place it's always been," he said.

A gust of wind blew away sand from underneath Patrick, revealing that he was sitting on the Krusty Krab's old sign.

"I'm sorry, Patrick!" SpongeBob said. "I'm sorry I let you down!"

"Don't apologize to me!" Patrick said. "Apologize to HIM!"

SpongeBob looked confused. "Him?"

Patrick pulled in his stomach, making a crease that looked like a mouth. Then his stomach spoke! "If I don't get a Krabby Patty soon, I'm going to eat you AND your friend!" it growled.

Horrified, Patrick cried, "He's joking! He's got a really great sense of humor!"

But Patrick's stomach turned into a huge mouth and started gobbling up the Krusty Krab sign. Patrick screamed!

SpongeBob and Plankton ran back to their time machine and climbed in. "Well, the GREEN button didn't work, so let's try the RED one!" Plankton said, pushing it.

VRROOM! WHIRRR!

The time machine disappeared!

Once again, SpongeBob and Plankton hurtled through time and space. When they opened the photo booth curtain, they peeked out and saw . . .

. . . nothing. Everywhere they looked, they saw gray nothingness.

"Uh-oh," SpongeBob said. "This still looks like the future!"

He and Plankton stepped out of the time machine and found themselves in a great hall. They cautiously followed a long corridor. At the end of the corridor, they could see a mysterious hooded figure standing with his back to them.

They approached the figure. "Excuse me, sir," SpongeBob asked politely. "Could you tell us WHEN we are?"

Without turning around, the figure spoke in a low voice. "Who dares disturb the One Who Watches?"

"The One Who Watches?" SpongeBob said.

"Your name is The One Who Watches?"

"No!" the hooded figure said. "My true name is . . . BUBBLES!"

The figure turned around. It was a dolphin!

"Bubbles?" Plankton said, laughing. "What kind of a name is Bubbles?"

The hooded dolphin drew himself up with great dignity and said, "It is my ancient dolphin name."

"What's a dolphin doing out in the middle of space?" SpongeBob asked.

Bubbles looked out the window. "My kind have been watching and protecting the galaxy for ten thousand years."

SpongeBob suddenly understood. "So YOU'RE the one keeping the meteors from hitting us!"

Bubbles nodded solemnly. "Yes, I am. I could really do with a toilet break. Would you mind keeping an eye on things?"

"Sure thing!" SpongeBob said. Then he thought of something. "WHAT am I keeping my eye on?" he called after the dolphin.

But Bubbles had already left, closing the bathroom door behind him. SpongeBob walked over to the window and stood still, staring.

"What are you doing?" Plankton asked, tugging SpongeBob's arm.

"I'm watching," SpongeBob answered.

"But you don't even know what you're watching FOR!"

"Well, like, meteors! And black holes! And . . . more meteors!"

As SpongeBob stared out the window, two planets orbited into view. "Wow, there sure is a LOT to watch. Maybe we should split up the workload." He pointed to the two planets. "You watch the one with the big red eye and I'll watch the one with the ringy thingies. Like a team!"

As SpongeBob and Plankton watched, the two planets slowly moved toward each other.

"Okay, mine's moving," Plankton observed.

"Mine too!" SpongeBob added.

"This doesn't seem right," Plankton said. "Should we call Bubbles?"

"Let's give him a minute. He's been holding it for ten thousand years."

BOOM! The two planets crashed into each other and exploded! Little pieces of the planets fell all around Plankton and SpongeBob. "I'm pretty sure THAT wasn't supposed to happen!" SpongeBob gasped. "C'mon, Plankton! We've gotta clean this up before Bubbles gets back!" He tried to sweep the debris under the carpet with a broom.

Bubbles came back. "Ah, much better, yes," he said, smiling. "You two are free to go. . . ." But then he noticed the dirt and pebbles on the floor. He also noticed SpongeBob's broom. "What have you done?" He looked up in the sky. "What happened to Saturn and Jupiter? You were supposed to keep them from smashing into each other!"

"Sorry!" SpongeBob said.

"Now I'm going to lose my job!" Bubbles cried. He stared at SpongeBob and Plankton. "And YOU will lose your LIVES!"

Bubbles fired lasers at SpongeBob and Plankton! *ZAP! ZAP!* They turned and ran away, screaming. They headed for the time machine.

"Quarter me!" SpongeBob yelled. Plankton tossed him a quarter, but SpongeBob missed it! It landed near the time machine.

SpongeBob and Plankton dove into the machine. SpongeBob reached out, snatched the quarter, and dropped it into the slot. *VRROOM! WHIRR!*

Inside the time machine, Plankton said, "Okay, so the RED button wasn't right, either. . . ."

"Let's be scientific about this!" SpongeBob said. He stared at the complicated control panel. "Eeny, meeny, miney, mo!"

He pushed a button. *VRRRRROOOOMMM!*

Back in the not-very-distant past, Past SpongeBob walked into Mr. Krabs's office. He gasped when he saw the open safe. "Plankton?" he said.

Past Plankton heard SpongeBob and turned around, knocking over the fake formula bottle with the real formula bottle. "SpongeBob!" he cried.

FLASH! The time machine appeared in a burst of light, distracting Past Plankton and Past SpongeBob.

Plankton stepped out of the time machine.

"Plankton?" asked Past SpongeBob, confused.

SpongeBob stepped out of the time machine.

"SpongeBob?" asked Past Plankton, equally confused. "Who are you two supposed to be?"

"I'm you, from the future," Plankton explained.

SpongeBob pointed toward his past self with his thumb. "And I'm HIM, from the future."

"So you traveled back through time to help me?" Past Plankton asked. "Great thinking!"

SpongeBob shook his head. "Nope," he said. "He's helping ME!"

"But he's the enemy!" Past SpongeBob gasped.

"WAS the enemy!" SpongeBob corrected. "Now we're a TEAM!"

"A what?" Past Plankton asked. "A *tee-am*?"

"A TEAM!" Plankton corrected him. He turned to SpongeBob. "All right. Go get the formula!"

"All right, Plankton!" his teammate answered. SpongeBob ran toward the safe.

Past SpongeBob couldn't believe what he was seeing. "What have I become?" he asked.

CHAPTER 17

As SpongeBob groped in the safe, trying to take the bottle with the secret formula from Past Plankton, his past self talked to Plankton.

"Do you have flying boatmobiles in the future?" he asked.

"We only came back from the day after tomorrow, nitwit," Plankton said scornfully.

"Did they outlaw clothes in the future?" Past SpongeBob asked.

"No!" Plankton snapped.

"Then why are you naked?"

"Because they don't make clothes in my size," Plankton explained.

SpongeBob kept trying to grab Past Plankton, but Past Plankton dodged him.

"Hold still, you!" SpongeBob said in frustration. "Stop moving!"

"Are there rocket packs?" Past SpongeBob asked.

Plankton turned to SpongeBob. "Hey! Hurry up over there!"

SpongeBob quickly made a big grab for Past Plankton but accidentally knocked over the secret formula bottle.

"Uh-oh," Plankton said. "That ain't good."

An alarm went off. *BWHOOP! BWHOOP! BWHOOP!* "Initiating lockdown sequence," announced a computerized voice.

"C'mon, SpongeBob!" Plankton shouted. "We gotta get out of here!"

"Got it!" SpongeBob exclaimed as he grabbed a bottle from the safe.

"Come on!" Plankton yelled.

They ran into the time machine. *VRROOM! WHIRRR!* In a flash, the time machine disappeared.

Inside the photo booth, SpongeBob said, "That was crazy!"

"So THAT'S what teamwork is!" Plankton said, finally getting it. They high-fived.

"Priceless!" SpongeBob said, laughing.

Plankton looked at the bottle, taking in its beauty. "All those years I tried to make you mine. And I finally did it. I mean, WE did it."

● ● ●

In Burger Beard's book, a picture showed Sponge-Bob and Plankton high-fiving. "'And so,'" Burger Beard read to the seagulls, "'it would seem that our heroes had accomplished what they had set out to do.'"

While he read to the seagulls, Burger Beard steered his ship.

"Yay!" one of the seagulls cried. "Now, THAT'S an ending! SpongeBob wins!"

"Aren't you glad we tore out that cruddy one you had before?" another seagull asked.

But Burger Beard dropped the book onto the deck and said, "Oh, no. THAT'S not the end. LAND HO!"

The pirate steered his ship up onto the shore and kept going! His ship had wheels on the bottom! Burger Beard drove his ship through a crowded beach, forcing all the sunbathers to scatter.

"I'm coming!" Burger Beard shouted. "Okay, all you lazy people, OUT OF MY WAY!"

The beachgoers were confused. Why was this pirate driving his ship across the sand?

"Out!" Burger Beard shouted. "Out of my way!"

"Slow down!" the seagulls shrieked. "You're going too fast!"

He steered his ship straight into a parking place between two food trucks. "YES!" he yelled, satisfied to have found a spot that suited his plan perfectly.

Burger Beard turned to the seagulls. "All right, you feathered rats," he snarled. "Time to shove off!"

The seagulls looked at each other. Why had the pirate changed from a nice man who read them a story to a mean guy who told them to shove off?

"Why?" asked one of the seagulls.

"Well, I can't have you pooping all over my restaurant, can I?" Burger Beard answered.

"Restaurant? I thought this was a pirate ship!" the seagull said.

"Oh, it is," Burger Beard said. "But it's also my very own food truck! You know, like a restaurant on wheels!" As he said this, the pirate opened hatches, turned on a stove, and tied on an apron. His ship had indeed turned into a food truck: THE BURGER-MOBILE!

"Well, we're not leaving until we see how the story ends!"

Burger Beard thought for a moment, then said, "No problem. You guys like a little snack while you wait?"

"Sure! I'll take a curdled milk!" one hungry seagull said.

"How about a fish head?" another asked.

"And French fries covered in sand!"

The pirate reached into his food truck, pulled out a tray, and said, "Who wants some HOT WINGS?"

The seagulls drew back, horrified.

"Hey, wait a minute," one of them said. "Where's Kyle?"

"Which one of you is NEXT?" Burger Beard growled.

"Let's get out of here!" cried one of the seagulls. They all flew off, terrified.

Burger Beard chuckled. He heard a toilet flush, and turned to see the door of a tiny portable potty open. Little Kyle came out.

"Where did evewybody go, Mistew Piwate?" Kyle asked innocently.

"BOO!" yelled Burger Beard.

Kyle shrieked and flew away.

Laughing a loud pirate laugh, Burger Beard turned back to his food truck and got to work on his evil plan. . . .

CHAPTER
18

*I*nside the Krusty Krab, hungry customers sat around waiting for Krabby Patties that never came. Patrick sat at a table, famished. "Squidward!" he called for the millionth time.

"Still out of Krabby Patties," Squidward said automatically.

SHLURP! Patrick licked a photo of a Krabby Patty. "Does anyone have a picture of ketchup?" he asked.

Sandy ran into the restaurant with a wild look in her eyes and announced, "I done FIGGERED it out!" All the starving customers turned and stared at her.

She jumped onto a table. "We have angered the sandwich gods! Only a SACRIFICE will appease them!"

"Well, that sounds reasonable," commented one of the angry customers.

"Soon our post-apocawhatchamacallit will be

over, and Krabby Patties will RAIN DOWN from above!"

Mr. Krabs frowned. "Rain down? Well, THAT's no good. How will I get me money?"

A tough guy pointed at Mr. Krabs. "You don't like that idea? Then we'll sacrifice YOU!"

"No!" Mr. Krabs cried, drawing back. "You don't want a crusty old crab like me! How about Squidward?"

"We'll sacrifice HIM, too!" the tough guy said.

"Well, anything's better than working in this dump," Squidward said.

The angry mob surged forward, grabbed Mr. Krabs and Squidward, and carried them out of the Krusty Krab. Mr. Krabs and Squidward screamed!

FLASH!

Suddenly, the time-traveling photo booth appeared out of thin air!

Astonished by the sight of the time machine, the mob dropped Mr. Krabs and Squidward. Then the crowd parted as SpongeBob and Plankton emerged from the photo booth.

"It's not a good idea to have a sacrifice on an empty stomach!" SpongeBob said. He held up the bottle he'd grabbed from the safe. "Who wants . . . a KRABBY PATTY?"

The starving crowd cheered! "HOORAY!" they shouted.

"SpongeBob!" Mr. Krabs cried. "Is that . . . ME FORMULER?" Overjoyed, he rushed to his loyal fry cook. "Oh, happy day!"

Mr. Krabs grabbed the bottle and kissed it. "I missed you so much!" Then he asked SpongeBob, "Where was it? Where'd you find it?"

SpongeBob smiled modestly. "Well, Plankton and I built a time machine out of an old photo booth. And then we added . . ."

"CHEESE!" Patrick said, sitting in the booth, smiling for the camera.

"PATRICK, NO!" SpongeBob cried.

Too late. *VRROOM! WHIRR!* The time machine vanished in a flash!

Mr. Krabs addressed the crowd of hungry customers. "It's okay, everyone. The post-apocalypse is almost over! Ain't that right, SpongeBob?"

Mr. Krabs triumphantly reached into the bottle, pulled out the piece of paper inside, unrolled it, and started to read. "'Eugene: Eat my subaquatic air bubbles. Love, Plankton.'" Mr. Krabs groaned.

Plankton wheeled on SpongeBob. "You grabbed the wrong bottle!"

"How was I supposed to know there were two

bottles?" SpongeBob asked, shocked.

"Because there are ALWAYS two!" Plankton screamed. "The real one and the decoy!"

"I'm sorry, Mr. Krabs!" SpongeBob cried.

Mr. Krabs tossed the rude note from Plankton aside. "That's okay, SpongeBob. We'll just have to sacrifice the two of YOU!" He turned to the hostile mob. "Prepare them for the sacrifice!"

FLASH! The time machine reappeared!

Patrick stepped out. "I bring a message from the dawn of time!"

"What is it, Patrick?" SpongeBob asked.

"RUN!" Patrick shouted.

He took his own good advice as a SQUID-WARDOSAURUS REX burst out of the time machine, destroying it!

"A Squidwardosaurus rex!" Squidward cried. "For a prehistoric monster, he's terribly handsome!"

The dinosaur stomped through what was left of the Krusty Krab. The angry mob fled. The beast tore the remains of the restaurant apart.

"Gee, that's exactly what I'VE always wanted to do," Squidward said admiringly.

Still mad about bringing back the wrong bottle, Plankton glared at SpongeBob and growled, "NOW what do we do?"

"Well, Plankton, I guess we failed to accomplish our goals."

"WE?"

"But even failure hurts a little less when you do it as a team. Right?"

"THIS IS ALL YOUR FAULT!" Plankton yelled.

"Ooooooooh," the crowd said. Even the Squidwardosaurus rex stopped its rampage to watch the fight between Plankton and SpongeBob.

"My fault?" SpongeBob asked.

"YOU'RE the one who stole the wrong secret formula!" Plankton said accusingly.

"I didn't know there were two bottles!"

"OF COURSE YOU DIDN'T! BECAUSE YOU HAVE COTTON CANDY FOR BRAINS!"

"Ooooooooh," the crowd said again.

Plankton turned to them. "No, seriously. He really does."

"Well, we wouldn't even be in this mess in the first place if you weren't so selfish and evil!" said SpongeBob.

"Wrong! I WAS selfish and evil until you ruined everything with your teamwork."

SpongeBob gasped.

"You are the WORST TEAMMATE EVER!"

Plankton ranted. "I wish I'd never sung that stupid song with you!"

"You take that back!"

"Come on! Let's sing it again!" Plankton said sarcastically. He started singing, "TEAM JERKS! TEAM JERKS! TEAM JERKS!"

"Stop it!" SpongeBob cried.

But Plankton just kept singing. "TEAM JERKS! TEAM JERKS! TEAM JERKS!"

"STOP!" SpongeBob screamed, kicking over a trash can.

"OOOOOH!" the crowd said for the third time.

SpongeBob grabbed a recycling bin, dumped it, and mixed up everything on the floor.

"Oh, my Neptune!" said one shocked citizen. "He's mixing garbage and recycling!"

Panting and gasping, SpongeBob noticed everyone staring at him. He looked at himself. "Look at me! Why, I've become like all of you—savage, fear-ridden, and selfish!"

The angry customers looked at each other, feeling ashamed.

"An entire town full of formerly good citizens, turned into heartless freaks!" SpongeBob went on. "Bent on their own self-prever . . . uh, prehver . . ."

"Preservation?" suggested one member of the mob.

"YES!" SpongeBob said. "We've become alienated from each other, each one an island unto himself, concerned only with ourselves. And in the name of all fishhood, I am NOT about to let that continue!"

SpongeBob tore a piece of cloth off a handy fish's clothing and tied it around his head like a bandana. "And so if a sacrifice is needed to restore Bikini Bottom to its former glory, then I am willing to take one for the TEAM!"

Tears filled the eyes of all the citizens.

"You heard him," Squidward said.

The angry mob grabbed SpongeBob, lifted him over their heads, and carried him off!

CHAPTER 19

The crowd of angry customers chained SpongeBob to an altar shaped like a burger. "Sacrifice! Sacrifice! Sacrifice!" chanted the mob. Squidward put on a black executioner's hood and pulled on a rope, lifting a huge stone bun over SpongeBob. He tied the rope to hold the gigantic bun in place.

"Let the sacrifice begin!" announced Mr. Krabs.

The mob cheered! "And I thought MY friends were primitive," observed the Squidwardosaurus rex.

SpongeBob began to sniff. "Don't cry, me boy," Mr. Krabs said. "Everything's gonna be fine! For us, that is."

"I'm not crying, Mr. Krabs," SpongeBob said, sniffing some more. "I smell Krabby Patties!"

"That's right," Mr. Krabs said gently. "Keep thinking happy thoughts." He turned to Squidward and shouted, "NOW!"

Squidward swung an ax and cut the rope. The

heavy stone bun fell! SpongeBob braced himself, waiting to be squished . . .

. . . but nothing happened!

Mr. Krabs had jumped onto the altar and caught the stone bun! "The boy's right!" he announced. "I smell 'em, too! Someone somewhere is cookin' up one o' me original-formuler, world-famous Krabby Patties!"

With a loud grunt, Mr. Krabs tossed the big stone bun aside. Then he ripped off the leather clothes he'd been wearing ever since chaos had engulfed Bikini Bottom. "Okay, SpongeBob—go get it!"

"Wait," Squidward said. "You mean we can just take these uncomfortable clothes OFF?" He ripped off his leather clothes, too.

"Go find the Krabby Patty!" Mr. Krabs said to SpongeBob. "Come on, boy!"

SpongeBob followed the scent. "Let's go, everybody!" he said. "I've got some Krabby Patty orders to fill!"

Sniffing the air, he took off across the ocean floor. Mr. Krabs, Sandy, Patrick, Squidward, and the mob followed him.

"It's coming from over there!" SpongeBob cried as he led everyone up a hill.

But when they had almost reached the top of the hill, they all realized that SpongeBob was leading them up to the surface. The mob groaned. Sure, they wanted delicious Krabby Patties, but as sea creatures, they couldn't leave the water.

"All right," the leader of the angry mob said. "All secondary characters, come with me."

"Yeah," Squidward agreed. "I'm with you guys." He started to leave with the crowd, but Mr. Krabs stopped him.

"No way, Squidward. You're going up there with us."

"My feet hurt," Patrick complained.

"Patrick, you don't HAVE feet," SpongeBob pointed out.

Patrick gasped. "It's not fair! Sandy has feet! Squidward has feet!"

"Actually, I have FOUR feet," Squidward said.

Patrick sat down with a grunt. SpongeBob walked up to him and put his hand on his shoulder. "Patrick, it's not about feet."

"What IS this about, then?" Squidward asked.

"It's about being a TEAM and sticking together no matter WHAT!" SpongeBob said. As he was speaking, trying to inspire the others, no one saw Plankton hide inside SpongeBob's sock.

Squidward raised his arms in disbelief. "The only way we're going up there is if some sort of fairy godmother shows up and helps us breathe air!"

The words were scarcely out of Squidward's mouth when . . . *FLASH!* Bubbles the dolphin appeared in a flash of bright light! He floated right in front of them.

"Bubbles?" SpongeBob asked.

"You KNOW this guy?" Squidward asked in disbelief.

"Please don't hurt us, Bubbles," SpongeBob pleaded. "We're sorry we got you fired!"

"HURT you?" Bubbles exclaimed. "I've traveled back through time to THANK you. I'd been stuck in that job for eons. I needed a change, but I was too afraid to go for it."

SpongeBob grinned. "Glad we could help!"

Bubbles said, "And now it is MY turn to help. I can get you safely to the surface. Quick, all of you— jump into my mouth!" He opened his mouth wide.

"Come on, guys!" SpongeBob said enthusiastically. "Let's go!" He hurried into Bubbles's mouth.

But the other four hesitated.

Squidward said, "There's NO WAY I'm climbing into some dolphin's mouth!"

"Yeah, this guy just wants a free lunch!" Mr. Krabs agreed.

From inside the dolphin's mouth, SpongeBob pleaded with his friends. "Guys, if Bubbles has the courage to quit his dead-end, nowhere job and travel back through time to help us, then WE need to have the courage to—"

But before SpongeBob could finish his stirring speech, Bubbles swallowed the four of them all at once.

Inside Bubbles's head, the five friends were jammed together. "I never thought I'd be eaten by a dolphin!" Mr. Krabs groaned.

"No, if he was EATING us," SpongeBob corrected him, "he'd be chewing us up and we'd be going down there!" He pointed down the dolphin's throat. "THIS is what you call riding in style!"

"Not a lot of legroom in here," Squidward complained.

"Well, maybe if you didn't have FOUR feet," Patrick said.

Without anyone noticing, Plankton peeked out of SpongeBob's sock. "Note to self," he muttered quietly. "Never stow away in a gym sock."

Above them, Bubbles's blowhole opened wide. The chamber began to shake. "What's happening?" Patrick cried. "I feel tingly!"

Bubbles leapt out of the ocean. Then he blew the five friends out of his blowhole in a magical beam of energy!

"YAAAAAHHHH!" they screamed as they flew through the air.

CHAPTER 20

WHOMP! SpongeBob, Patrick, Mr. Krabs, Squidward, and Sandy hit sand, hard. They had landed on a beach. Magical energy crackled away from their bodies.

"Ow! My neck!" Squidward moaned.

Bubbles floated in the air above them. "I have done all I can. The rest is up to you!"

"Thank you very much, Bubbles!" SpongeBob called, waving.

"Farewell, SpongeBob!" Bubbles said. "Now to update my resume!"

The dolphin rocketed into the sky and disappeared through a portal that closed behind him.

Down on the beach, Sandy took off her helmet and breathed in the fresh air. "Ahhh," she sighed. "Sweet not-from-a-tank air! Oh, how I've missed you!"

The others took deep breaths through their noses. Squidward wrinkled his. "This place smells awful!"

"I smell a Krabby Patty!" SpongeBob said, sniffing. "It's coming from over there! Come on, team—let's go!"

SpongeBob led the way. They immediately saw that the beach was covered in sweaty human sunbathers. "I have a bad feeling about this place," Mr. Krabs warned.

Patrick stopped next to a man's foot. To Patrick, the foot seemed gigantic—like a whole creature. "Maybe this guy can help us. He looks smart. He's got FIVE heads!"

SpongeBob politely addressed the foot. "Sir? Could you tell us where to find a Krabby Patty?"

No answer. Then they heard a snore. SpongeBob saw the rest of the sleeping man. "A giant hairy porpoise! It's beached! It's suffering! Poor thing . . ."

Sandy tried to tell the sea creatures about human beings. "Y'all, those aren't porpoises, they're—"

"All hands on deck!" Mr. Krabs cried, ignoring Sandy.

"Oh, brother," she said, giving up.

"We need to get these guys back in the water!" Mr. Krabs said, waving his claws, directing the others to help him.

"C'mon! PUSH!" SpongeBob said.

The five teammates lined up along one side of

the sleeping sunbather and started to push. "Heave!" shouted Mr. Krabs. "Ho!" cried the others. They managed to flip the man onto his face.

"Heave!" shouted Mr. Krabs. "Ho!" cried the others. They flipped him onto his back.

They tried to flip him again, but they were getting tired. The man fell back onto them. From underneath the man, Squidward said, "Well, I guess THIS is where that horrible smell was coming from!"

They tunneled their way into a sand castle and climbed up to the top, where they met a little girl.

"Whoa!" said the surprised girl when she saw the five friends.

"Excuse me," SpongeBob said. "Do you know where we can get a Krabby Patty around here?"

A shadow fell over the sand castle. The girl's big brother had arrived. When he saw the four sea creatures and Sandy, he yelled, "Invaders!"

"Uh-oh," SpongeBob said.

"You get out of my sister's sand castle!" the boy shouted. He kicked the castle, sending the friends flying in different directions.

Patrick landed on a little girl's ice cream. To him, it was a GIANT ice cream cone! "Where have you BEEN all my life?" he asked. Then he dove into the ice cream, eating his way through it.

Squidward landed on the slippery, oily back of a sunbather. He tried to walk up her back, but he kept sliding in the suntan oil.

The little girl spotted Patrick in her ice cream cone. "GROSS!" she cried, flinging the cone away with Patrick still in it. The cone hit Squidward and knocked him off the sunbather's back. He and Patrick landed in the sand several feet away. "Hey, Squidward!" Patrick said happily, ice cream still around his mouth.

SpongeBob and Sandy landed on an umbrella. "Sandy!" SpongeBob said. "The Krabby Patty! I think I see where the Krabby Patty smell's coming from!" He tried to run off the umbrella, but it collapsed on the man underneath it. When the man opened the umbrella, SpongeBob and Sandy flew through the air and landed in a postcard rack next to Mr. Krabs.

Patrick and Squidward climbed up the rack to join them. "Hey, SpongeBob!" Patrick called. "Did you find the giant ice cream?"

SpongeBob climbed to the very top of the rack and sniffed the air. "Hey, team!" he said. "I smell Krabby Patties! I think they're THAT way!"

He led them onto a sidewalk. But then they looked up and SCREAMED!

A bunch of bicyclists, skaters, pedestrians, and skateboarders were speeding right toward them!

*T*he team scrambled out of the way just in time.

"Now what?" SpongeBob asked.

"We're never gonna make it!" Squidward groaned.

SpongeBob looked around for a solution and spotted . . . a bicycle!

With SpongeBob and Patrick working the pedals and Sandy, Mr. Krabs, and Squidward on the handlebars, they were able to make the bicycle glide right along. To humans on the sidewalk, the bicycle looked like it was moving without a rider.

When a mother with a baby stroller saw the bike, she stopped and stared. Mr. Krabs frantically rang the bike's bell—*BRRING BRRING! BRRING BRRING!*—but the mother didn't budge. So Mr. Krabs jumped from one bike handle to the other, tipping the bike just enough to make it swerve and miss the woman with the stroller.

Unfortunately, that sent the bike straight toward

a surfboard leaning against a truck. The bike zoomed up the surfboard and flipped upside down!

"YAHOO!" Patrick whooped.

They all flew off the bike and landed in a toy wagon. *WHUMP!* The five team members peered up over the edge of the wagon and saw . . .

. . . BURGER BEARD'S BURGERMOBILE!

A sign read HOME OF THE KRABBY PATTY. A long line of customers snaked away from the little order window.

"What the . . . ?" Mr. Krabs exclaimed.

"'Home of the KRABBY PATTY'?" SpongeBob read in utter disbelief.

The customers eagerly devoured the burgers as fast as they were served up. Mr. Krabs read a smaller sign. "Eight ninety-nine for a Krabby Patty? Why didn't *I* think of that?"

Inside the Burgermobile, Burger Beard was grilling up Krabby Patties, happily humming to himself. He heard a voice say "YOU!" accusingly.

It was Mr. Krabs. He was standing on a window ledge with SpongeBob, Patrick, Sandy, and Squidward, looking angry. "Cease and desist that unauthorized patty-flipping!"

"Yeah!" SpongeBob added. "That's MY job!"

Burger Beard dropped his spatula. "How did you

get here?" he asked, astonished. "You can't leave the water and breathe air!"

"Well," SpongeBob explained politely, "there was this magical dolphin from the future who shot us out of his blowhole, and now—"

"Wait!" Burger Beard interrupted as he flipped the pages of his book. "That's not in the book! There's no magical dolphin in this story. . . ."

Mr. Krabs looked confused. "Book? What story?"

Burger Beard grinned, showing a mouthful of rotten teeth. "The story of how Bikini Bottom was brought to its knees when its beloved Krabby Patty formula was stolen by ME, Burger Beard!" He laughed an evil, sickening laugh.

Patrick sat down to listen. "How does it end?" he asked eagerly.

Burger Beard looked in his old book. "Well, let me see," he said slowly. "It looks like Burger Beard becomes the richest food-truck owner in all the land."

"But how did you steal the formula?" SpongeBob asked.

Burger Beard shrugged. "It was easy. I simply rewrote the story. And . . . *poof!* Secret formula!" He held up the bottle for them to see. They all gasped.

"Me formulcr!" Mr. Krabs croaked.

"You rewrote the story?" Squidward sneered.

"That makes no sense. I'm not buying it."

"Fine!" Burger Beard said. "I'll show you!"

He pulled out a feather pen and wrote in his moldy old book, reading out loud as he wrote. "'The brave and handsome Burger Beard BANISHED our poor heroes to become STRANDED on Pelican Island.'"

Energy began to swirl around SpongeBob, Patrick, Sandy, Squidward, and Mr. Krabs. "YAAAAH!" they all screamed.

And then they vanished!

"'The END!'" Burger Beard said, laughing as he slammed the book closed.

Pelican Island was a bleak, rocky island in the middle of the ocean. The five team members huddled on a gray rock while pelicans screeched and flapped around them. When a pelican clapped its beak near his nose, Squidward yelped.

"This looks bad," SpongeBob said, worried. "And these guys look hungry. LOOK OUT!"

A pelican buzzed over their heads.

"Nice," Squidward said sarcastically. "So this is what teamwork gets you."

"Here!" Mr. Krabs called to the pelicans. "Take Squidward, ya vile beasts!"

Patrick slumped on the rock. "I wanna be on a NEW team," he whined. "This one's broken!"

SpongeBob turned to Sandy, desperate for a solution to their predicament. "Sandy!" he said encouragingly. "You're smart! Do you have any ideas?"

"I ain't been too smart since I found this ol' piece

of paper," Sandy said bitterly. She pulled out the page from Burger Beard's book that said THE END and threw it down.

Plankton popped up from SpongeBob's sock, looked at the paper, and laughed an evil laugh. No one noticed.

SpongeBob thought hard and got an idea. As the pelican buzzed over their heads again, SpongeBob plucked a feather from its tail.

"Ouch!" cried the pelican.

"Now all we need is some ink," SpongeBob said. He looked down at the rock near Squidward's feet. "Which Squidward has helpfully provided!"

Squidward looked embarrassed. "It happens when I'm nervous," he explained sheepishly.

SpongeBob dipped the sharp tip of the pelican feather into the puddle of Squidward's black ink.

"Whatever yer gonna do, make it quick!" Mr. Krabs urged. "They're closin' in on us!"

"I'm gonna write us an ENDING!" SpongeBob said.

"Will it be a happy ending?" Patrick asked.

SpongeBob nodded and smiled. "It's going to be SUPERPOWERED!"

He used the feather pen to write on the piece of paper from Burger Beard's book. When he finished writing, glowing bands of energy swirled around him, Patrick, Sandy, Mr. Krabs, and Squidward. Then they vanished in a burst of energy that scattered the pelicans!

The page SpongeBob had written on still lay on the rock. Plankton crawled out from his hiding place behind a stone and read the paper. Then he grabbed SpongeBob's feather pen. "I'll show you a happy ending," he said, chuckling evilly.

Back at the Burgermobile, Burger Beard was inside his food truck, flipping Krabby Patties. Outside, customers enjoyed the delicious food.

In the air above the beach, a swirling energy portal opened. The customers looked up to see what was happening.

Four superheroes flew out of the portal! Thanks to the ending SpongeBob had written on the page, he, Patrick, Mr. Krabs, and Squidward were human-sized superheroes with incredibly muscular bodies and awesome powers! SpongeBob was THE INVICI-BUBLE! Patrick was MR. SUPER-AWESOMENESS! Mr. Krabs was SIR PINCH-A-LOT! And Squidward was SOUR NOTE!

SpongeBob, Mr. Krabs, and Squidward landed on their feet and struck heroic poses. Patrick posed facing the wrong way. "Da-da-da-DA!" he sang heroically.

"Patrick!" SpongeBob hissed. Patrick turned around and faced the right way.

The crowd stared at them.

Burger Beard stuck his head out the ordering window to see what was going on. SpongeBob said, "We'll take one secret formula . . . TO GO!"

"But . . . but I BANISHED you!" Burger Beard stammered, amazed to see them back.

SpongeBob turned to Squidward. "We need to clear the area, Sour Note! You know what to do!"

Squidward put his hands together and his clarinet assembled itself right in his hands! He took a deep breath and blew. *SQUOOORKKK!*

When they heard the hideous sound of Sour Note's clarinet, everyone on the beach doubled over and covered their ears. Screaming, they ran away.

Burger Beard ran out of his food truck to stop the people from leaving. "Wait! Wait! WAIT! HOLD ON! No! No! Me customers!"

Sour Note stopped playing. SpongeBob said to Patrick, "Mr. Superawesomeness, take him down!"

Patrick closed his eyes and concentrated. Two ice cream cones flew out of a couple of kids' hands and went straight to Patrick. Clouds formed overheard as Patrick raised the two ice cream cones to the sky.

Then he lowered them and licked both cones at the same time.

"Um, maybe we should've picked a better superpower for you, Patrick," SpongeBob admitted.

Burger Beard ran back to his truck, where he grabbed his old book and a feather pen. "Let's see you get outta THIS one!"

When he saw what Burger Beard was going to do, SpongeBob gasped and turned to Mr. Krabs. Mr. Krabs launched one of his claws at Burger Beard, pinning his hand holding the pen to the side of the truck.

"Huh?" Burger Beard said. He thought of a simple solution. "All right, then," he said, switching the pen to his other hand.

But Mr. Krabs fired his other claw, pinning that hand, too!

So Burger Beard took the feather pen in his mouth and tried to write in his magical book that way.

"Get ready for the Invincibubble!" SpongeBob cried. He took a deep breath and blew a HUGE bubble out of the wand on his helmet.

The bubble rocketed toward Burger Beard and snagged the magical book from his pinned hand, carrying it away. "NO!" Burger Beard cried, struggling against the two claws holding him captive.

SpongeBob turned to face Squidward, Patrick, and Mr. Krabs. "All right, team! Time for 'hands in the middle'!"

Unfortunately, to do hands in the middle, Mr. Krabs had to call back one of his claws, which freed one of Burger Beard's hands. The pirate used his free hand to pry open the remaining claw and escape!

Mr. Krabs put one of his claws on SpongeBob's hand. Patrick and Squidward put their hands in, and then all four hands were covered by a giant squirrel hand!

It was Sandy!

The big squirrel struck a few poses and did some cool karate moves. "You can call me . . . THE RODENT!"

Patrick looked around. "Hey, the pirate isn't here. Where'd he go?"

They all turned to look, and saw that the Burger-mobile was gone! All that remained was Mr. Krabs's other claw, slowly spinning on the ground.

"Oh, no!" Mr. Krabs cried.

CHAPTER
23

SpongeBob looked around for clues that might reveal where Burger Beard had gone. He spotted a pool of golden liquid on the ground. "Aha!" he cried.

He ran his finger through the puddle and licked his finger. Then he smacked his lips, nodding. "It looks like Burger Beard forgot the first rule of mobile fry-cooking: always batten down your grease traps!"

SpongeBob pointed to a trail of golden liquid leading away from the spot where the Burgermobile had been parked. "Follow that grease, team!" Mr. Krabs shouted as his superhero suit sprouted jet engines.

Mr. Krabs rocketed down a street that ran along the beach. Sandy sprinted behind him with Squidward on her back. Patrick brought up the rear, riding on SpongeBob's back as he propelled himself with his powerful bubble-blower!

On his Burgermobile, Burger Beard peered

through a spyglass until he spotted the floating bubble with his old book trapped inside it. "Thar she blows!" he called, laughing.

But when he looked in his rearview mirror, Burger Beard saw the heroes gaining on him. Growling, he release his side sails. The sails gave him more speed, and he shot ahead.

"Engage boosters!" Mr. Krabs said, firing up extra engines.

"Hang on tight, Squidward!" Sandy whooped. "YEE-HAW!"

But it was SpongeBob and Patrick, cruising on bubble power, who reached Burger Beard first. Patrick climbed on board but accidentally sent SpongeBob spinning away. SpongeBob managed to grab Patrick's shorts, pulling them down until he could see Patrick's butt crack. "AHH!" SpongeBob screamed.

Burger Beard dropped his heavy anchor, knocking SpongeBob and Patrick off the Burgermobile. "Arr, arr, arr, arr!" he laughed like the evil pirate he was.

He spotted the book in the bubble floating above his ship-truck. Letting go of the steering wheel, Burger Beard climbed up into the crow's nest. He was so eager to get his magic book back that he didn't notice SpongeBob, Patrick, Mr. Krabs, Sandy, and Squidward standing on his anchor, behind the Burgermobile!

"He's after the book!" SpongeBob yelled, pointing. "Sandy, use your squirrel powers!"

"Roger that!" Sandy replied. She ran up the anchor's chain and onto the Burgermobile.

But as SpongeBob watched anxiously, Burger Beard got closer and closer to his magic book. "She's never gonna make it!" he cried.

He spotted a large metal statue just ahead on the right side of the road. "Everyone, LEAN!" he shouted. They all leaned to the right, and the anchor hooked on to the statue.

The Burgermobile jolted, and Sandy fell right off. "Whoa!" she shouted. But the Burgermobile didn't stop. It kept going, dragging the heavy statue behind it. Mr. Krabs, Squidward, SpongeBob, and Patrick were sent flying into the street. Burger Beard managed to hold on to the mast.

As the Burgermobile slowly came to a halt, Burger Beard grabbed for the book in the bubble!

"The book!" SpongeBob said. "Sour Note!"

Squidward blew his clarinet. The clarinet's horrible sonic wave popped the bubble, and the book fell down into the truck.

"NOOO!" Burger Beard howled. He jumped

down into the truck just in time to see his precious book burst into flames on the grill. "NOOOOOOO!"

SpongeBob, Patrick, Squidward, and Mr. Krabs strode up to the pirate. "All right, Burger Beard," SpongeBob warned. "Prepare to be teamworked. GET HIM, THE RODENT!"

Sandy filled her cheeks with nuts from a handy bin and fired them at Burger Beard. But the wily pirate batted the nuts away with his spatula until she ran out of them. "Aw, nuts!" Sandy said. "I'm all out of nuts!"

Burger Beard used a rope to hoist himself up into the crow's nest. Patrick summoned dozens of ice cream cones to fly at him, pointy end first.

"Patrick, I should NEVER have doubted your powers!" SpongeBob said admiringly.

Burger Beard jumped out of the crow's nest and swung around on a rope. The ice cream cones followed him. But when he swerved back up, the ice cream cones all headed straight for Patrick! He fell to the ground, covered in ice cream.

"I can't think of a sweeter way to go," he moaned.

Burger Beard dangled the secret formula in his hand. "It's ALL MINE!"

"Not so fast, *Booger* Beard!" Mr. Krabs said. He shot his claws at the mast, cutting it into three pieces.

The pirate fell to the deck and dropped the formula, which rolled into the street. Mr. Krabs's claws flew back to his arms.

"Me formuler!" Mr. Krabs shouted. But before he could grab it, Burger Beard shot him away with a blast of melted butter!

SpongeBob reached for the formula, but Burger Beard saw him. The pirate pulled on a lever. Hatches opened on the Burgermobile and REAL CANNONS popped out!

"Voilà!" Burger Beard said proudly.

"Uh-oh," SpongeBob said. A cannonball was rocketing towards him!

CHAPTER 24

Using his incredible flexibility, SpongeBob managed to dodge all of Burger Beard's cannonballs. One flew right through SpongeBob's bubble wand and came out trapped in a bubble. He watched the cannonball float away.

"Huh?" he said. Then he got an idea!

While Burger Beard continued to fire cannonballs at him, SpongeBob used his bubble wand to catch every single one in a bubble, rendering each cannonball harmless!

"They're beautiful!" Patrick said. He reached up to touch one floating over his head. *POP! WHAM!* The bubble popped, and the cannonball fell on Patrick, knocking him out cold.

"Patrick!" SpongeBob called to his friend. *BLAM!* Distracted, SpongeBob failed to dodge Burger Beard's last cannonball, which sent him flying. The pirate laughed a long, loud, evil laugh.

SpongeBob lay on the ground with cannonballs falling from bubbles all around him.

Still laughing his evil laugh, Burger Beard grabbed the secret formula and ran back to his Burgermobile.

Covered in ice cream, Patrick crawled over to SpongeBob and cradled his best buddy's head. "SpongeBob!"

"Patrick?"

"Yeah, buddy. Talk to me."

"I'm . . . I'm seeing a bright light."

Patrick moved his head to block the sun, which was shining right in SpongeBob's eyes. "Is that better?' he asked.

"Much. Thank you," SpongeBob said. "But the discomfort I feel in my eyes is nothing compared to the shame I feel for letting down the Patty. For letting down Bikini Bottom."

"Yeah, SpongeBob," Patrick said, nodding. "You really blew it."

"No, Patrick. WE blew it . . . as a team."

"Nope. This one's on you."

Inside the Burgermobile, Burger Beard hummed happily as he started the engine. "Hmm-hmmm, tiddly hmmm . . ."

Suddenly, a loud voice boomed through the food truck. "Where do you think YOU'RE going?"

Burger Beard looked around and saw . . . Plankton!

The mean old pirate laughed hysterically. "Why don't you get goin', little fellow, before you hurt yourself?"

Burger Beard put his Burgermobile in gear and hit the gas, but the vehicle wouldn't move. When Burger Beard looked around again, he saw the reason.

Plankton now had a huge, strong body! He was holding one end of the truck up over his head. He shifted his hands and lifted the entire Burgermobile over his head!

"Plankton?" SpongeBob asked when he saw the new version of his teammate.

"It's Plank-TON!" Plankton roared. He flipped the Burgermobile upside down and shook it. Burger Beard screamed as he fell. He managed to snag the broken mast and climb up into the ship-truck through a trapdoor in the deck.

Plankton growled, flipped the ship right-side up, shook it, and spun it around. Inside, Burger Beard was pinned to the wall by the force of Plankton's spinning. Kitchen knives flew at Plankton, narrowly missing him.

Plankton's huge red eye peered through the window of the Burgermobile. "Come out, come out, wherever you are. . . ."

Burger Beard squeezed hot sauce straight into Plankton's eye!

"MY EYE!" Plankton screamed. He threw the food truck down onto its side, and Burger Beard jumped out and ran down the street.

"He's getting away!" SpongeBob yelled.

Plankton jumped out from behind the ruined Burgermobile. "Ready for a Plank-TON of bubbles?" he asked.

SpongeBob smiled and nodded. Plankton picked him up, took a deep breath, and BLEW through SpongeBob's bubble wand. A massive cloud of bubbles headed for Burger Beard.

The pirate looked back and saw an avalanche of bubbles bearing down on him. He tried to run, but slipped and slid so much on the soapy bubbles that he ended up running in place. Plankton reached down and picked him up by the hat.

Holding Burger Beard in one hand, Plankton held out his other hand and said, "The secret Krabby Patty formula, please."

"Come on!" Burger Beard pleaded. "Team up with ME! We'll be RICH and POWERFUL!"

SpongeBob and Patrick gasped. Would Plankton accept the pirate's offer?

CHAPTER 25

Plankton shook his head. "No, thanks," he told Burger Beard. "I'm already part of a teamwork."

He moved his hand closer to the pirate. Burger Beard gave him the bottle that held the secret formula. Plankton drew back his muscular foot and punted the pirate far, far away.

"YAAAAAH!" Burger Beard screamed as he flew through the air. He returned to the deserted island where he'd lost all his treasure, buried up to his neck in sand. A seagull landed on his bare head. Burger Beard moaned.

Back on the boardwalk, Patrick asked, "Can we do hands in the middle again?"

"Yes, we can, Patrick!" SpongeBob agreed. "But this time, there's ONE MORE HAND to go in the middle!"

SpongeBob put his hand in. Patrick put his on top

of SpongeBob's, followed by Mr. Krabs's, Squidward's, and Sandy's.

But where was Plankton's?

"Plankton?" SpongeBob asked, looking for their last team member.

Plankton was standing nearby, staring at the secret formula in his hand. The secret formula he'd been trying to get ahold of for so many years.

"Hmm . . . ," he said, thinking.

"Oh, no!" Mr. Krabs gasped, thinking Plankton was going to keep the formula for himself.

Plankton handed the bottle to Mr. Krabs. "Here you go, Krabs. She's all yours."

Mr. Krabs joyfully took the bottle. Then he looked suspicious. "This doesn't have another insulting note in it, does it?"

"No," Plankton said. "That's the OLD me, the one who turned his back on everything important just to have that formula all to himself. But I realize now that keeping something to myself is . . . selfish."

"Especially when that something is the Krabby Patty," SpongeBob said, smiling proudly. He turned to the other team members. "Okay, everybody! Let's get back to Bikini Bottom and put things back the way they were."

Suddenly, he realized something awful. "Oh, no!" he cried. "I don't have the page from Burger Beard's magic book! It must be back on Pelican Island!"

"Don't worry," Plankton reassured him. "I thought of everything." He handed the last page of the book to SpongeBob. "All right, SpongeBob. Take us home!"

"Thanks," SpongeBob said. He looked around for Squidward and saw him admiring his own superhero body.

"Oh, yeah," Squidward said. "Nice."

"C'mon, Squidward!" SpongeBob called. "It's time to go back and open up the Krusty Krab!"

Squidward looked appalled. "Are you out of your MIND? I'm NEVER leaving this place! I mean, look at me! I'm a GOD!"

"No, Squidward," SpongeBob corrected. "You're a CASHIER."

SpongeBob started to write on the page from the magic book.

"Wait a minute!" Squidward cried. "What are you doing? NO!"

Energy swirled around them and they vanished!

Back in the Krusty Krab, Squidward appeared behind his cash register, back to his normal self. "Well, it was fun while it lasted," he said, sighing.

Mr. Krabs, Sandy, Patrick, and SpongeBob reappeared. They, too, were back to normal.

"Don't be sad, Squidward," SpongeBob said. "I left you a little surprise, under your shirt."

Squidward lifted his shirt, and was delighted to see . . .

"Rock-hard abs?" he said, amazed. "Aw, SpongeBob, you're okay in my book."

"Shucks!" SpongeBob said modestly.

"Excuse us," said an eager voice. They all turned to see a huge line of customers snaking out the door of the restaurant.

"We'd like three thousand Krabby Patties, please," said the customer at the front of the line.

"That must mean things are back to normal," Squidward said.

SpongeBob zipped into the kitchen and returned with a tray full of sandwiches. "Who wants three thousand Krabby Patties?" he asked.

The customers all cheered!

"First one's for you, Gary," SpongeBob said as he handed a Krabby Patty to his pet snail. "Extra mayo, just the way you like it."

"Meow," Gary said, looking pleased.

"AHA!" SpongeBob shouted. "Caught you red-handed! Gary HATES mayo . . . PLANKTON!"

SpongeBob opened Gary's shell, revealing Plankton hidden inside, operating a robot version of the snail. "Up to your old tricks again already, eh?" SpongeBob said.

"Hey, I'm just putting things back the way they were!" Plankton said innocently.

The real Gary crawled up next to SpongeBob. "What do you have to say about this, Gary?" asked SpongeBob.

"GRRROWWWLLL!" Gary roared.

"Oh, shrimp," Plankton said. Moments later, he was riding his robot snail out the front door of the Krusty Krab, screaming. Gary chased him out, still roaring.

As he watched Plankton ride away, SpongeBob waved goodbye. "See you later, *tcc am*matc!"